THE SWALLOW HOUSE SUMMER

When Issy Dillaine discovers she was adopted as a baby, she sets out to discover all she can about Amy Grant, her birth mother. She never dreamt her quest for the truth would lead her into a world of Z-list celebrities — as well as the arms of investigative journalist Ed Stanwood. But Ed's uncle Jonathan Jackson was the QC who had headed up the prosecution team working to convict her mother of fraud . . .

Books by Margaret Mounsdon
in the Linford Romance Library:

THE MIMOSA SUMMER
THE ITALIAN LAKE
LONG SHADOWS
FOLLOW YOUR HEART
AN ACT OF LOVE
HOLD ME CLOSE
A MATTER OF PRIDE
SONG OF MY HEART
MEMORIES OF LOVE
WRITTEN IN THE STARS
MY SECRET LOVE
A CHANCE ENCOUNTER
SECOND TIME AROUND
THE HEART OF THE MATTER
LOVE TRIUMPHANT
NIGHT MUSIC
FIT FOR LOVE
THE POWER OF LOVE

MARGARET MOUNSDON

THE SWALLOW
HOUSE SUMMER

Complete and Unabridged

LINFORD
Leicester

First published in Great Britain in 2014

First Linford Edition
published 2015

Copyright © 2014 by Margaret Mounsdon

A catalogue record for this book is available
from the British Library.

ISBN 978–1–4448–2445–2

Published by
F. A. Thorpe (Publishing)
Anstey, Leicestershire

Set by Words & Graphics Ltd.
Anstey, Leicestershire
Printed and bound in Great Britain by
T. J. International Ltd., Padstow, Cornwall

This book is printed on acid-free paper

1

The aircraft rose above the clouds, leaving the Celtic Sea of southwest Ireland far behind. The Fasten Seat Belts sign was illuminated but Issy had more important things on her mind than turbulence. As her fellow passengers settled down she opened her bag and extracted an envelope.

The newspaper cutting was tattered and yellowed with age and she knew the contents by heart, but she couldn't help re-reading the caption underneath.

Someone had raised a hand to obscure the photographer's lens. All Issy could make out was a blonde-haired woman, her face hidden from the camera, being hustled into a police station.

Issy closed her eyes. Until two months ago she had believed Pat and Molly Dillaine to be her parents, even though it had always struck Issy as strange that she resembled neither of them in appearance or character.

Pat was a burly, red-haired bully who believed women should be kept in their place, and Molly, his wife, was a petite, sparrow-like woman who would dart around obeying Pat's orders without protest.

Molly tried to persuade Issy to wear pretty dresses and girly bows in her hair, and bake cakes. Neither ambition met with success. Issy was a tomboy. She wanted to travel and see the world.

'I'd like to work for an airline,' she'd announced one day over lunch after she'd seen an advert in the newspaper.

'That figures,' had been Pat's terse reply.

Issy had wondered why her father had taken against such an innocent comment. Now she knew why. Amy Grant, the blonde woman in the newspaper, had worked for an airline. She was also Issy's mother.

While she had been growing up other

things had puzzled Issy. Her childhood had been spent in a remote cottage on the Dingle Peninsula, with spectacular views over the bay. The only source of social life was the neighbouring village; but visits there were discouraged, as were casual callers.

When Issy's grandparents came to stay, Molly would spend days baking, airing beds and washing curtains. Issy was always sent away during their visit, with a terse 'Do as you're told' from her father when she protested.

'We don't have a spare bedroom, so they must have yours,' was all Molly would say by way of explanation as she packed Issy's case, before Pat drove her down to the convent school where she would board until her grandparents had left.

'What about your family?' Issy had dared to ask her mother one day. 'Don't they want to see me either?'

'Hush with your questions,' Molly replied. 'You know how they upset your father.'

Whenever there was any mention of England Pat would abruptly change the subject.

'I was born in England,' Issy would object, but to no avail. If she made more of a scene she would be sent to bed without any supper.

Her birth was yet another thing that confused her. Why had she been born in a place called Redhill, when her parents never travelled further than the local town once a month to stock up on groceries?

'We had folks there,' Molly admitted one day.

'I thought you had no family,' Issy said.

'I meant I had no family in this country,' Molly corrected herself, with an agitated glance at Pat.

'So we're British?' Issy asked.

'We're Irish and don't you forget it,' Pat growled. 'Now go get some logs.'

Issy had seen the way other fathers played with their children. They bought presents on their birthdays and arranged treats. Pat did none of these things.

'Don't have money to waste on fripperies,' he mumbled whenever Issy asked for anything.

Yet that didn't stop him lavishing money on his pride and joy, a Black Shadow motorbike. The bike was his only indulgence and when he wasn't out on his boat, he would spend hours working on it.

Strangely, Issy's childhood wasn't an unhappy one. She loved being out in the fresh air, and during the summer months she would explore the archaeological sites and talk to the visitors. They came from all parts of the world and she loved hearing stories of their homelands, lands she one day longed to visit.

Occasionally she would earn extra pocket money helping out at the dig; money she kept well-hidden from her father.

During the winter, when it was too cold to go out, she would lose herself in a world of books.

One thing her parents couldn't stop her doing was reading. There was a big library at school and the English mistress encouraged Issy's love of language.

'It's not everyone I'd let take books home,' Miss Thompson would say, 'but I know you'll treat them well and bring them back.'

'I will, Miss Thompson, I will,' Issy promised, clutching the latest offering to her chest, stroking the cover.

She devoured every book she borrowed even if the subject matter wasn't to her taste. Her favourite reading was biographies about people who overcame tremendous odds to fulfil their dreams. Issy marched with the suffragettes, tears pouring down her face when she read how they were eventually granted the vote. She read of the brave men and women who lost their lives for the sake of their country. When nothing else was to hand she would read about faraway lands. She'd look at the map on the wall at school and wonder if she would ever visit England again, the land of her birth.

She had discovered Redhill was in the county of Surrey, south of London, and she imagined it to be a leafy, sunny place where it never rained and people lived in heated houses.

Life may have been quiet on the peninsula but it was never dull. Pat made sure Issy did her fair share of chores around the cottage; and of an evening, when Molly took in dressmaking, Issy helped her mother sew on buttons or hem the seams. It was a companionable time, and with Pat working on his bike outside it was one of the few occasions when Issy felt close to Molly.

Then, last November, everything had changed.

The previous summer Molly had caught a summer cold. It had gone to her chest and, weakened by years of hard work in harsh conditions, she had been unable to fight off the infection.

After her funeral, Issy had moved away from the cottage to the city of Cork. Her father had not been happy about it, but Issy had been determined and he hadn't been able to stop her. She loved the bright lights and the adrenalin rush of working in a modern office. After years of existing with basic amenities she soon adapted to modern technology, and although she rented a tiny bedsit she wouldn't have swapped her room for anything. She bought a painting of a Persian bazaar to hang on her wall, and covered the sofa with brightly-coloured cushions to hide the gaps where the stuffing poked through. She spent her weekends exploring the city and socialising with her new friends. She was a popular girl and never short of a date.

Every day was different, and being on the front desk of an information technology company was a rewarding job. Her naturally cheerful disposition was an asset to her employers and she loved the challenges of her new life:

meeting different people; going on courses; learning modern business methods and Internet skills.

'The boss wants to see you,' her colleague Maire informed her when she came back from lunch one Friday afternoon.

A frisson of apprehension worked its way up Issy's spine. Like everyone else, the company was making cutbacks. Was that why she was being called upstairs?

Maire cast her a sympathetic look. Were her thoughts running along the same lines? Now she'd glimpsed the bright side of life, Issy couldn't bear the thought of returning home to work as Pat's unpaid drudge.

'How do I look?' Issy asked, straightening her uniform blouse and tucking it into the trousers of her pale grey suit.

'Put your jacket on,' Maire advised. 'It looks more businesslike.' She straightened Issy's name badge. 'Good luck,' she whispered, and watched Issy walk towards the lift, where the elevator swept her up to the top floor.

The carpet was so deep in the executive suite that her feet sank into the pile. Issy had only been up here once before. It had been on her first day when she had been personally introduced to Mr Stocker. His handshake had almost crushed her fingers, but she had felt an immediate liking for an employer who wanted to know every member of staff by name.

'Go right in,' his personal assistant said as Issy approached her desk on trembling legs. She could tell from the concerned look on the girl's face that it wasn't good news.

Mr Stocker wasn't the only person in his office. The senior Human Resources manager was present.

'Why don't you sit down, Issy dear?' Mrs Bowler came forward with a kindly smile.

The words went over Issy's head as Mr Stocker explained what had happened. There had been an accident on the coast road. Her father had crashed his motorbike. The police suspected the sun might have temporarily obstructed his vision. No other vehicle had been involved.

★ ★ ★

Shock had numbed Issy's grief, and she had gone about her various official tasks as if in a trance.

Mr Stocker had been more than generous in allowing her time off, and his wife had made a room available in their house for Issy to sleep over, insisting she wouldn't take no for an answer and that she could stay for as long as she liked.

It was well into the New Year before Issy felt able to return home to clear out her parents' effects. It was then she learned that her parents didn't actually own their cottage.

'I hate to push you, Ms Dillaine,' the landlord apologised over the telephone, 'but I'm converting the cottage to a holiday let and I've already taken Easter bookings. I'll need time to get things ready beforehand.'

'I understand,' Issy assured him. 'Give me a day or two?'

The cottage seemed smaller than she remembered. The landlord had driven her up from his office in order for her to sort through her parents' possessions.

'I'm afraid they didn't even own the furniture,' he informed Issy, with an embarrassed expression on his face, 'but there are some private things I thought you might like to go through. Give me a call when you're finished and I'll drive you back.'

Locked away in a tin box under a pile of logs, Issy discovered the papers that were to change her life.

2

It had been a while since Ed had seen his uncle. Jonathan Jackson QC had moved up in the world after he had taken silk, and his legal career had gone from strength to strength. Although his relationship with his sister, Ed's mother, was cordial, contact between them was infrequent.

Ed's mother had been happy in her job as a dinner-lady, and his father had enjoyed working for the railways. As such, their social paths rarely crossed. Ed couldn't remember the last time he had seen his aunt or his cousins; not that he ever gave the matter much thought.

'I expect you were surprised to hear from me,' Jonathan began after they had shaken hands.

'You could say that,' Ed replied, sinking into the deep leather sofa. All around them he could hear the discreet murmur of club conversation. 'How are you enjoying retirement?'

After his long and distinguished career, Jonathan had finally hung up his wig two years ago.

'I play a little golf, do some community work and sit on one or two committees, that sort of thing.'

'But it isn't enough?' Ed hazarded a guess.

'Some days are longer than others,' Jonathan admitted, 'but I've never been one to complain. Thank you, Henry.' He accepted his whisky from the waiter. Ed did the same, then picked up a handful of peanuts and chewed them thoughtfully. His uncle never did anything without a reason, and Ed was wondering what this meeting was really about.

'How is the world of investigative journalism?' Jonathan asked, sipping his whisky.

'Much the same.'

'I read your latest exposé. It was

good. In fact, it was more than that. It was brilliant.'

'Thank you,' Ed accepted the praise with a deprecating smile, 'although it was a team effort.'

Ed and his colleagues had exposed a particularly unpleasant financial fraud that had made the headlines, and for a while he had been doorstepped by the regular press, all wanting an exclusive. Never one to seek the limelight, he had been pleased when the fuss had died down and his life had returned to some semblance of normal.

'What are you working on now?' Jonathan asked.

'I've one or two ideas in the pipeline.' Ed hedged around a direct reply.

He didn't like being under-employed, and lately he had begun to get itchy feet. That was the main reason he had answered Jonathan's summons to meet him at his club. It had been something to do on a dull January day when he had nothing in his diary, but already he was questing the wisdom of accepting the invitation. He had forgotten how manipulative his uncle could be, and he was pretty certain Jonathan hadn't invited him here to play family catch-up.

'What's this all about, Jonathan?' he asked.

Ed was finding the atmosphere in the bar stifling. He looked longingly out of the window. There had been a smell of snow in the air as he walked up from the tube station to the elegant eighteenth-century townhouse, home to his uncle's club. The biting January wind had frozen his cheeks, but he would have preferred being outside and feeling the sting of icy rain on his face to being stuck in the overheated atmosphere of a stuffy bar.

'I have developed a hobby. It helps to pass the time and I have a commission for you.'

Jonathan Jackson now had his nephew's full attention.

'Oh yes?'

'Do you remember Amy Grant?'

Ed frowned. 'Refresh my memory.'

'It's difficult to know where to start,' Jonathan admitted.

'How about at the beginning?'

'Amy Grant,' Jonathan recalled with a smile, 'was one of those people who light up a room. She was blonde, beautiful and had huge blue eyes.'

'And?' Ed wondered where this was going.

'Have you heard of Don Dealy?' Jonathan asked, with an abrupt change of subject.

'You mean that personality who runs talent shows on television?' A look of disgust crossed Ed's face. 'The man's a monster.'

'I suspect his behaviour is part of a very clever act.' A wry smile twisted Jonathan's lips.

'All the same . . . ' Ed shuddered.

'Amy Grant was a frequent guest at his place in the country — Swallow House. He still lives there.'

'How long ago was this?'

'Over twenty years. He used to hold

parties, very fashionable at the time. Everyone who was anyone would fight to get an invitation, until the scandal broke and they dropped him like a hot potato.'

'It's coming back to me now. I remember reading up on the investigation; something to do with credit cards?'

'Amy and Don Dealy were implicated.'

'An unpleasant business.'

'There was not enough evidence against either of them, and Don went to ground until the fuss died down, but once the dust settled he bounced back. These days he's achieved establishment status.'

'What was Amy's part in all this?'

'She was implicated because she worked as a hostess in an exclusive VIP Lounge for one of the airlines.'

'Go on,' Ed urged his uncle.

'The people behind the scam were never caught. It was alleged they were guests at one of Don's parties.'

'And Amy's involvement?'

'Some of the credit card links were traced back to her. It was a flimsy piece of evidence and wouldn't have stood up in court, but the establishment wanted to make an example of someone.'

'And she was in the wrong place at the wrong time?'

'Precisely.'

'What happened to her?'

'The investigation collapsed, and she too disappeared from public view.'

'A sad story,' Ed said. 'So what's this hobby you're talking about?'

Jonathan produced a briefcase and extracted some papers, which he nudged towards Ed.

'I found this advertisement on my iPad. I'm ashamed to admit that these days I linger over a second cup of coffee at breakfast, and it caught my eye.'

'*Anyone with information about Amy Grant,*' Ed read out loud, '*please contact Issy Dillaine at the following box number.*' He put it down on the table. 'Amy Grant is a common enough name. It doesn't have to be *your* Amy Grant.'

'It is,' Jonathan replied with conviction.

'How do you know?'

'Her daughter was called Isadora.'

'Amy had a child?'

Jonathan nodded.

'And the father?'

'Amy was a single parent.'

'There's no record of the father?'

'Not as far as I know,' Jonathan replied. 'There was a rumour that she had been married, but I don't know . . . ' He shrugged.

'It still doesn't mean this Issy Dillaine is Amy's Isadora.'

'Amy's daughter was adopted by Pat and Molly Dillaine.'

'Adopted?'

'Part of my duties as a junior in the original enquiry were to log all details about witnesses, or anything else I thought pertinent. It was part of my training before I went on to bigger and better things.'

Ed hid a smile. Jonathan was nothing if not immodest, and if he was expecting Ed to agree with him he was going to be disappointed.

'This was in the days before ready computer access, you understand?' Jonathan continued when Ed didn't respond.

Again Ed nodded.

'One day I came across a snippet in an Irish newspaper. Amy had been involved in a car accident. She had been living in Ireland with some distant relations.' Jonathan raised his eyebrows as if to make sure Ed was following.

'Who were called Dillaine?'

'Exactly.'

'I still think it's a long shot that this Isadora is Amy's girl.'

'Maybe, but I haven't finished my story.'

A niggle of unease began to work its way up Ed's spine. 'Why do I have the feeling I'm not going to like what you're about to say?'

'I answered the advert.'

'Why?'

'In your name,' Jonathan added in a rush.

'What?' Ed jerked upright, knocking his knee against the table, scattering peanuts all over the floor.

His uncle waved away a hovering waiter.

'You have an appointment to meet up with Issy Dillaine this afternoon at two, under the clock at Victoria Station.'

'I don't believe this. You had no right to use my name. What story did you give?' Ed demanded.

'Yours.'

'Mine?'

'What better? If she runs a check on you she'll see your background is impeccable, and she'll believe you're a journalist sensing a sensational scoop by proving her mother's innocence for once and for all.'

'Aren't you forgetting one thing?'

'What's that?' Jonathan asked.

'Issy may not know about her mother's past.'

'Then use your charm to find out

what she does know. I'm sure that's not beyond your capabilities.'

'Why don't you do your own dirty work if you're so keen to find out about her mother?'

'Think about it, Ed. I could hardly give her my name. If she found out about my involvement in the original investigation, I would be one of the last people in this world she would want to talk to.'

'With good reason!'

Sensing victory, Jonathan glanced at his watch.

'You haven't much time, Ed so if you're interested I suggest you get going.' He opened his wallet and drew out several notes. 'Expenses.' He passed them over.

'You should have consulted me about this before you decided to use my name.' Ed glared at his uncle.

'I know, but I also know you can't refuse a challenge; and you've got to admit, this could be an interesting assignment.'

'Doing what, exactly?'

'Finding out what you can about all that really happened at Swallow House.'

'Why?'

'I felt at the time Amy got a raw deal. Bad publicity sticks, and she had it thrown at her by the bucketload.'

Ed picked up Jonathan's plastic folder.

'I've listed a few bits and pieces that might be of interest to you,' Jonathan said. 'Nothing official, a few details I can remember off the top of my head.' He raised his eyebrows questioningly.

Ed snatched the money from his uncle's hand.

'If this turns out to be a wild goose chase, I'll want more than expenses from you.'

'There's a story here. Take my word for it.'

'Is there anything else you're not telling me?' Ed demanded, his suspicions aroused.

'Not that I can think of right now,' Jonathan assured him. 'Let me know how you get on. I'm sorry you haven't time for lunch.'

'No thanks to you.'

'Don't grumble, dear boy.' Jonathan soothed his anxieties with an urbane smile that had won him many a case. 'You know how you hate the club scene. Racing around the countryside working against the odds is far more your thing. Who knows? You may even fall in love with this Issy Dillaine. It's about time you settled down with a proper female who can knock some sense into you.'

'Don't talk rot, Jonathan.'

Ed was breathing heavily. His head was in a whirl. Despite his protestations, there was something about this case that fired his imagination. An innocent young girl caught up in a web of subterfuge. Had she been made the scapegoat for somebody else's crime?

'One last thing,' Jonathan said.

'What?'

'I'd be grateful if you didn't mention my name.'

'I'm used to protecting my sources. Your secret's safe with me.'

'I knew I could rely on you.' Jonathan stood up.

Ed blinked. 'If Amy was innocent, what good would proving it do now?'

'It would clear her name; and that, I should imagine, is what her daughter is after.'

'And if her name isn't cleared?'

'Then at least Issy will know the facts. Put yourself in her shoes, Ed. Wouldn't you do the same?'

'I suppose I would,' Ed admitted.

'Give my regards to your mother. We must get together some time. Cordelia sends her love. She also said I wasn't to bully you into accepting my little commission.'

'Thank Cordelia for her good wishes. Unfortunately her wise advice seems to have fallen on deaf ears.'

With this parting shot Ed strode from the bar, through the reception and out into the cold January afternoon.

3

Ed took the steps two at a time and hurtled into the main concourse of Victoria station. He was over twenty minutes late. The tube doors had refused to close at Green Park and he'd sat in his seat fuming, wondering whether or not it would be quicker to walk the last part of the journey.

Would Issy still be waiting for him, and how on earth would he recognise her?

The more Ed pondered the matter, the more he wondered why he had listened to his uncle. He had better things to do than to rake up the past. Who was going to remember exactly what had happened at Swallow House after all this time? The world had moved on.

The concourse was the usual teeming mass of travellers. Tourists trundled suitcases behind them, clutching hotel details, looking lost. January was hardly a holiday month, yet a crowd of students, jabbering away in a language Ed didn't understand, impeded his progress as they clustered around their guide.

Apologising, Ed clambered over rucksacks and backpacks, something that looked like a tent and goodness knew how many anoraks, until he finally came to a halt under the clock near the departure board.

He looked round in exasperation. A flower seller, a retired military-looking gentleman collecting for charity . . . there was no female who remotely resembled his idea of what Issy Dillaine would look like. They had missed each other. Ed began to dial Jonathan's number to update him on the situation just as the overhead tannoy sputtered into life. Moving away from the loudspeakers and not looking where he was going, he collided with the luggage trolley.

The trolley shrieked in shock and grew legs. Ed realised the parcel he had grabbed to stop from falling over was actually a female swathed in a thick coat, stripy tights and stout boots. Her furry hat flew through the air and she sank to her knees as he released his hold. As she lay sprawled at his feet, Ed looked down into the face of the most beautiful girl he had ever seen in his life.

Her eyes were blue as periwinkles, and even though her hair had gone all spiky under her fur hat she didn't look ridiculous. Her complexion reminded him of ripe summer peaches, and her parted pale pink lips revealed perfect teeth. The overall effect was marred by the fact that she was looking at him as though he were something particularly unpleasant that had crawled out from underneath a stone.

'What the blazes are you playing at?'

There was nothing of the delicate flower about her language as she proceeded to tell him what she thought of big oafs using mobile telephones who didn't look where they were going.

'Are you hard of hearing as well as clumsy?' She raised her voice when all Ed did was blink at her. 'You must have been at the back of the queue when manners were handed out.'

The accent was soft Irish, even if the words were basically Anglo-Saxon.

'You aren't by any chance Issy Dillaine?' Ed croaked when he found his voice.

'What's it to you?'

'We had a date to meet up at two o'clock.'

'Is that why you've arrived at half-past?'

'Sorry.'

The blue eyes narrowed as she inspected his appearance. 'You're younger than I imagined you would be.'

Issy managed to make it sound as if that were also his fault as she struggled to her feet, ignoring Ed's outstretched hand.

He retrieved her fur hat. 'It's rather squashed.'

'It was all right before it came into contact with you. Same goes for me.'

'Would you like me to buy you a new hat?' he offered.

'I'd like you to tell me why you're so interested in Amy Grant.' Issy got straight down to business as she brushed dirt off her coat.

Ed did a quick inspection of the concourse. 'Could I buy you a coffee? I missed lunch.'

'I could use a sandwich,' she admitted reluctantly. 'I've been hanging around for ages. I thought I'd been stood up.'

'Blame my uncle.'

'Your uncle?' A puzzled frown wrinkled Issy's brow.

'I got delayed; you know, family duty?' Ed replied, remembering too late Jonathan's wish to remain anonymous. He stood up straight and did his best to look presentable. It was a social skill that had grown rusty after years of thrusting microphones under reluctant noses and demanding awkward questions of unwilling interviewees. 'Could we start again?' he pleaded.

'No more knocking me off my feet?' Issy's face softened a fraction.

'Scout's honour.' Ed returned her smile.

'In that case I accept your offer of a sandwich.'

It was a quiet time of day and they had no difficulty in finding a spare table in the steamy snack bar.

'I suppose I should introduce myself,' Ed commented as he returned with coffee and sandwiches.

'I know who you are. You're Ed Stanwood,' Issy replied. 'Your note said you were a journalist. So why do you want my story?'

Issy unwrapped one of the sandwiches Ed had purchased and took a healthy bite. She looked at him expectantly.

'I'm not sure.' Ed cleared his throat. 'First of all, may I know what your relationship to Amy Grant is?'

'She was my mother.'

'I take it we're talking about the same Amy Grant?'

'If you mean, was my mother the supposed fraudster Amy Grant, then yes.'

'So you know about that, do you?'

'I do, and I'll understand if you want to check out now and have nothing more to do with me.'

Issy was no longer smiling. There was coldness in the blue eyes as she surveyed Ed across the table. She stirred her coffee in a confrontational gesture.

'Ms Dillaine,' Ed began.

'You can call me Issy,' she said.

'Issy, then. In my line of work you often find things are not what they seem, and one of the first lessons I learned was not to be judgemental. I don't know your mother's full history, but whatever happened you should always be proud to be her daughter.'

Issy blinked at him and didn't speak

for a few moments.

'Thank you for that,' she eventually said in a hoarse whisper.

'And I can assure you I have no intention of walking out on you.'

Ed wondered where that statement had come from, but there was something about the way Issy was looking at him that was making it hard to think straight.

'Like me, you're stubborn,' she acknowledged with a wry smile.

'At last we agree on something.'

Her expression wrenched Ed's heart. Despite her robust stance, Issy looked vulnerable sitting opposite him eating her sandwich. Experience told him that right now she could do with a friend.

'What exactly do you want to know about Amy Grant?' he asked.

Issy finished her sandwich and pushed away her plate.

'Until recently, I didn't know Amy Grant was my mother. It wasn't until the people who I thought were my parents died, and I found some old papers, that I realised I had been adopted.'

'This was in Ireland?'

'How did you know that?' Issy demanded.

Ed knew he was going to have to tread carefully. That was twice now he had nearly put his foot in it.

'Your accent,' he improvised.

'Right.' Issy pondered for a few moments before she went on. 'My parents were distant relations of my mother's family. I came across some correspondence in a tin box after their deaths, and that's when I realised that until then I had been living a lie.'

'It must have been quite a shock.'

'And some,' Issy admitted.

'Do you know anything about your father?'

Issy shook her head. 'There was no mention of him.'

'Have you read up about the investigation?' Ed asked.

'A little, but I didn't really know what I was looking for. I was just getting over the shock of discovering I was adopted. Then I went online to do some research on one of those family tree websites — ' Ed nodded at Issy to go on. ' — where I discovered all about Amy Grant. Things don't get much worse than that, I can tell you.'

'And you think she was innocent?'

'I have no idea,' Issy admitted, 'but I would like to know what happened.'

'Why?'

'Because someone had a guilty conscience.'

'What do you mean?' Ed frowned at her.

'Pat and Molly Dillaine received an allowance every month to look after my needs.'

'From where?'

'England. I found an account and statements. The bank wouldn't give me any details, something to do with client confidentiality; but before you go thinking I'm a wealthy heiress, I should tell you Pat Dillaine spent the money on his Black Shadow motorbike.'

'They don't come cheap.'

'I've sold the bike now, and used the money for a flight to England.'

'Good move.' Ed approved.

'What's your take on things?' Issy asked.

'Until a few moments ago,' Ed revealed, 'I thought you might be wasting your time and that the wisest thing for you to do would be to have a holiday here then go back home.'

'What changed your mind?'

'Your anonymous allowance.'

'That trail's gone cold. The bank froze the account when Pat Dillaine died, and no further payments have come through.'

'There was no correspondence?'

'Just the bank statements.'

'Did you get any other responses to your advert?' Ed asked.

'I got one.'

'Who from?'

Issy searched in her bag for the letter.

'It was from a man in Kent, near Canterbury. Here we are.' She unfolded a sheet of paper. 'His name's Dealy, and he lives at Swallow House.'

'Don Dealy?' Ed demanded, careful to keep any excitement out of his voice.

'Swallow House was where it all happened, wasn't it?' Issy asked. 'And this Don Dealy was a minor celebrity?'

'He hosts a television talent-spotting show these days.'

'You're kidding!'

'Prime-time viewing. What does he say?

'He wants to meet up this weekend.'

'Will you go?'

'Of course.' Issy refolded the letter. 'Do you want the last sandwich?'

Ed looked down at the cheese on rye and shook his head. He wasn't one for intuition, but he was unable to prevent a shadow of dread casting a cloud over his day.

4

Don Dealy's country house was a long drive from the station, and Issy had been forced to empty her purse when the taxi driver demanded an extortionate fare.

'Gotta charge you both ways.' The driver made a show of apologising. 'I've the return journey to think of. An empty cab doesn't pay my bills, and with the price of petrol going up every day I'd be running at a loss.' He passed over his business card. 'Hope you enjoyed the ride. Can't drop you at the front door 'cos I'm nearly over my driving hours limit, and I don't want to run out of time. Ring this number when you want to go back.'

Deciding she would rather walk all the way back to the station than contact that driver again, Issy pressed the security button on the gate and gave her name. There was a buzzing noise, and a clipped voice instructed her to proceed to the house.

She set off down the drive. The frosty gravel crunched underfoot. She shivered, glad she had worn boots and her thick coat and thought to bring a torch. She arced the beam around the grounds. Strange shapes loomed out of the darkness. The hedges had been trimmed to within an inch of their lives and classic Greek statuettes graced the archways.

A loud splash nearby indicated water. She turned her torch in the direction of some reeds and caught a glimpse of a duck before it paddled away from the light.

The ghost of a smile softened Issy's cold lips. Don Dealy couldn't be that bad if he kept ducks, even though his taste in topiary and garden statues was a bit questionable.

She wondered what sort of welcome she would get, and what exactly he could tell her about her mother.

Although she didn't like being out on her own in dark and unfamiliar territory, she did not regret her decision to turn down Ed's request to accompany her. Something about the story he had spun didn't ring true. Her sixth sense told her he hadn't penned the reply to her advert. The language was far too precise for a modern, in-your-face reporter. Ed Stanwood was after more than merely a sensational story: of that, she was convinced.

When Issy had asked if Ed's interest in the case was professional or personal, he'd mumbled some sort of response regarding a scoop but hadn't looked her in the eye.

'I'd like to know how you get on with Don Dealy,' Ed had insisted as Issy pocketed the business card he handed her.

'Why, are you after an audition for this show of his?' she'd teased, determined to keep things on a light note.

A look of horror had spread over Ed's face.

'Perhaps not,' she'd agreed. 'Best stick to the day job. See you around.'

As she'd walked towards the bus station after their meeting, she'd felt Ed's eyes burning a hole in her back.

Issy had now reached the top of Don's drive. Several cars were parked in front of the house. A security light flooded the forecourt. Issy half expected a guard to tell her to freeze and hit the deck, before reminding herself that she had every right to be on the premises. Before her courage gave out she strode towards the substantial oak front door.

Issy's computer check on Don Dealy had revealed he had quite a reputation. Amongst other things, he was responsible for launching several successful media careers. His publicity shots showed a man confident of his own power and well used to being the centre of attention. There was mention too of his actress wife, Lucinda Whitby. She ran a theatre workshop and an annual youth arts festival, named in memory of her brother Finlay. Last year's theme had been 'equality'. Finlay, Issy discovered, had also been an actor.

Issy raised her hand to the knocker. It was an intricate wrought-iron affair, a carved bullfrog squatting on a lily pad, its plump body forming the basis of the knocker. She caught her breath in shock. She had found an identical pencil sketch of just such a door-knocker at the bottom of Molly Dillaine's tin box. Amy had signed off the drawing with a smiley face and a row of kisses.

Issy hesitated. This was her last chance to turn back. She straightened her shoulders. Standing on a freezing doorstep having second thoughts would not answer any of her questions, and she didn't intend to wimp out now. It was time to join the party. She rapped firmly on the knocker.

A maid answered the door and showed Issy into an upstairs bedroom.

'You can leave your coat here, madam.' She indicated a spare bed covered with an assortment of coats and wraps. 'The bathroom is through there, if you'd like to freshen up. You'll find everything you need. When you're ready, either ring the bell or you can make your way downstairs. The drawing-room is first door on the left.'

Issy shrugged off her coat and, going into the bathroom, peered at her reflection in the mirror. Her cheeks were pinched with cold and she had never felt less like a party in her life. She hoped the dress she had chosen was suitable to the occasion. It was a wrapover grey wool weave, which went well with boots.

Reapplying a bold bow of lipstick, she ran a comb through her tangled hair; then, still feeling grubby, she used some of the scented liquid soap to wash the grime off her hands. The train journey had been a long one and for the first half Issy had been forced to stand, crushed against a wheeled suitcase on one side and an active baby who kept grabbing fistfuls of her hair on the other.

Issy dried her hands on a fluffy white towel. She needed a few moments to get her head together before she went downstairs. She wondered exactly how well Don Dealy knew her mother. Was he the person who had set up an account in Issy's name; and, if so, why?

With these thoughts crowding her mind, Issy crept out into the corridor. The door to the room opposite was ajar, and she couldn't resist a peep inside. It was a nursery, and she could almost hear the echoes of a child's happy laughter. A coal fire burned in a far corner, and the reflection of the flames played on the red leather saddle of a dappled rocking horse. As a child, Issy had seen a craftsman carving a wooden horse at a trade fair, and ever since she had longed for one just the same. In her wildest dreams she imagined being given one as a present, perhaps on her birthday; but in her heart of hearts, she knew that was never going to happen.

She put out a hand and gave the

rocker a gentle push. The wood creaked and moved under her touch. It was as if the horse was inviting her to clamber onto its back.

A child's mobile, moved by the draught from the rocking horse, gently chinked above her head. The golden stars and crescent moons twirled and spun in the half-light. No expense had been spared with the room. Fairy-tale characters danced along the wall frieze, and soft dolls smiled at her from their shelf on the dresser. A toy train set had been laid out on the floor beside a miniature farmyard. The bookshelves were crammed and Issy's fingers itched to re-read all the children's classics she had enjoyed so much from the school library.

This was a room full of love. She could feel it all around her. Invisible hands gently pushed her backwards and forwards as she rode the rocking horse on an imaginary journey. This was her room. Destiny had guided her here tonight.

She threw back her head, enjoying

the happiness of the moment. The shadows on the wall seemed to be guiding her with their gentle movements. The sensation was so real it took Issy's breath away.

'What are you doing here?'

A voice shattered Issy's dreams. The shadows disappeared and her feet slipped out of the stirrups. She clutched at the little mane of hair to steady herself. A figure silhouetted in the doorway moved out of the shadow to reveal a man wearing an open-necked shirt and dark trousers. The steely grey eyes fixed on her never blinked. He advanced into the room. Nothing had prepared Issy for the strength of Don Dealy's magnetism.

'You invited me to your party,' she stuttered, wishing her shadowy friends hadn't deserted her.

'You still haven't answered my question.' He waited patiently for her reply.

'The door was open and I peeped in. My name is Issy Dillaine,' she introduced herself.

His expression gave nothing away as he put out a hand to steady the horse's rockers.

'You're Amy's daughter?

'Yes, I am.'

His voice softened. 'You're very like your mother.'

'Am I?' Issy's voice trembled.

'You must be about the same age as she was when I first met her.'

'I'm twenty-three,' Issy replied, but Don appeared not to hear.

'I'm so sorry for what happened,' he said with a look of intense sadness.

'Mr Dealy,' Issy broke in, but was forestalled by his raised hand.

'Don, please.'

'Don, then.'

His sadness turned to a smile. 'There, that wasn't so difficult, was it? What was it you wanted to know?'

'Why did you contact me?'

'It's a long story.'

From her perched position on the rocking horse, Issy looked down into Don's face. As a young man he must have been incredibly handsome, and the years had added a charisma that women of all ages would find hard to resist.

Don put out a hand to help Issy dismount. Again losing her footing in the tiny stirrup that had been made for smaller feet than hers, Issy laughed and stumbled into Don's arms.

A disturbance in the corridor caused him to turn so swiftly Issy nearly fell over.

'Darling,' he greeted the woman now standing in the doorway, 'I've found our missing guest. Issy, may I introduce my wife, Lucinda. Lucinda, meet Issy Dillaine.'

'Hello,' Issy smiled, 'it's nice to meet you.'

'She's Amy's daughter,' Don added.

The blue eyes flickered in Issy's direction and for a moment she thought she detected fear. Without acknowledging her presence, Lucinda turned back to Don.

'She shouldn't be in here. This is the

nursery. Take me back downstairs.' Lucinda linked her arm through her husband's. 'If we don't eat soon, dinner will be ruined.'

Don's eyes met Issy's over Lucinda's bowed head. With an apologetic smile he shepherded his wife from the room; leaving Issy, feeling like a chastised schoolgirl, to trail after them.

5

'Hey, Issy,' a fresh-faced girl from Killarney called over from the pigeon-holes. 'Did you have a good weekend?'

'Fine.' Issy did her best to smile.

Don had been the perfect host, charming and considerate. He wouldn't hear of Issy going back to London before they'd had a proper chance to talk, but Lucinda had hardly left them alone together for a moment.

'You've got a letter,' the girl from Killarney waved it under Issy's nose, 'with an Australian postmark. Are you thinking of moving on?'

'Not yet.' Issy took it and thanked her.

The rooms at the hostel were neat and clean, but lacked much privacy; and with everyone surging around, gossiping and catching up on their news, it wasn't until later that Issy was able to read her letter. She slit open the envelope and glanced at the signature. It was from someone called Roger Street.

I knew an Amy Grant, Issy read, before I moved to Australia. If we are talking about the same Amy Grant, she was very dear to me. I am not planning a trip to Europe in the foreseeable future, but my younger half-brother Harry Willetts lives in England and I am sure he would be pleased to meet up with you. Please contact him. I know he would love to hear from you. Maybe once we've established contact we could Skype?

Dialling the number Roger had given, Issy waited impatiently for someone to pick up her call.

'Hello?' a breathless male voice answered.

'Harry Willetts?'

'Who?'

'This was the number I was given,' Issy began.

'Sorry, of course. Yes. Hi, er — who is this?'

'My name is Issy Dillaine.'

'I don't know you, do I?'

'Your brother asked me to contact you.'

'My brother?'

'Roger Street is your brother?' Issy began to grow annoyed, fearing she might have been the victim of a hoax.

'Rog, of course. How is he? I must get down to Oz to see him sometime. Trouble is, it's such a long way away.'

'I've never met your brother,' Issy began to explain.

'You haven't? I thought you said you knew him.'

'He wrote to me.'

'Did he?'

'About my mother?'

'Sorry, you've lost me there.'

'He suggested we should meet up.'

'What for?'

'Hasn't he been in touch with you?'

'I've been a bit busy recently. Haven't really caught up with my contacts. Does Rog want me to take you out to dinner? I might have a window some time next week. Why don't you call back?'

Issy's patience ran out.

'There's no need to go to any trouble on my behalf. I'm sorry to have wasted your time.'

'No, don't hang up.' There was urgency now in Harry's voice. 'Did you say Issy Dillaine?'

'Yes.'

'There's a message on the corkboard. One of the guys must have taken it. It's from Roger. It says: *Please look after Issy Dillaine for me. She's a dear friend and currently in London.*'

'Roger said I was a dear friend?' Issy frowned in puzzlement.

'What say we meet up? Hold on, let's talk dates. How about tomorrow?'

'I thought you were busy all week.'

'I've been stood up. Would you believe it? The girl practically begged for a date and now she's sent me a 'take a hike' text. Well, *she* can go take a hike as far as I'm concerned. Meet you at Ollie's, seven o'clock?'

'Where?'

'It's a wine bar. Ask anyone. They'll know where it is. Ciao.'

He rang off. Stifling a sigh, Issy checked her own texts. There were several missed messages from Ed Stanwood. She rang his number.

'Want to come round?' he asked. 'I'm doing lasagne.'

Issy's only sit-down meal all week-end had been dinner on Friday evening. Lucinda had made frequent apologies to her other guests about the dried-up chicken, explaining that things had been delayed due to Issy's late arrival, increasing her discomfort to such an extent that her appetite deserted her.

'Sure it's not too late?'

'My Sauce Edouard is to die for,' Ed coaxed. 'Three cheeses and anchovy? I always make far too much for one.'

'I'll get a bottle of wine.' Issy leapt off

the bed, glad not to have to spend the evening moping in her room. 'See you soon.'

* * *

The address Ed had given her was on the second floor of a converted warehouse.

'This is lovely.' Issy looked round the surprisingly tidy flat. She gazed out of a huge picture window at the panorama of a dying winter sun casting its rays on the Thames. The huge red ball sank slowly from sight, creating a red wash of colour in its wake. The water gradually turned into an inky reflection of the deep purple sky. 'It reminds me of home, the sun setting on the water.'

'It's quite a sight, isn't it?' Ed stood beside her, holding two glasses of chilled white wine. He offered her one. 'One of the best free shows in town; and that's something coming from a native-born Yorkshireman.'

He indicated two steaming portions

of lasagne already served up on the breakfast bar.

'Eat first, talk later?'

After they'd finished supper Issy carried her glass of wine over to the sofa. Ed drew the curtains and adjusted the lighting.

'Let's have some music,' he suggested, 'get a bit of atmosphere going?'

He sat down beside her.

'So, catch-up time?'

'Who's going first?' Issy asked.

'Better be you,' Ed replied. 'How did you get on with the infamous Don Dealy?'

'You don't like him, do you?'

'I don't like what he does to people on that show of his.'

'You're not a fan of talent shows?'

'I don't like to see people humiliated in public.'

'They put themselves up for it,' Issy said.

'And you think they deserve to have their dreams dashed?'

'That's not what I was saying,' Issy insisted.

'Isn't it?'

'It's Dan's job to be controversial. Aren't you guilty of that sort of thing too?'

'No, I am not,' Ed protested.

'You want readers, he wants viewers. Where's the difference? It's entertainment by another name, that's all.'

'I can see you've kissed the Blarney Stone,' Ed acknowledged with a wry smile.

'You're just not used to having your views contested.'

'Look, can we postpone this spirited difference of opinion to another time?' Ed enquired. 'We do have more important things to discuss.'

'I suppose we do.'

'Tell me about Lucinda Whitby, Don's wife,' he suggested, before Issy could get in another crack about unscrupulous reporters.

'She wasn't exactly welcoming,' Issy acknowledged, 'but Don was the perfect host.'

'He's always had an eye for the ladies.'

Issy rolled her eyes. 'There was no chemistry of that sort between us. Besides, he's years older than me.'

'I shouldn't let him hear you say that.'

'Well, he is.'

'His publicity handout says he's forty five.'

Issy made a noise of disbelief at the back of her throat. 'Then I'm sweet sixteen! But I suppose he could be attractive to ladies of a certain age. He's got that way of looking at you that makes you think you're the most interesting person in the world. I used to meet lots of Irishmen like that back home, but *they* didn't spend hours under the sunlamp topping up their tan or colouring their hair.'

'Ouch. Does nothing escape your eagle eyes?' Ed enquired, refilling their wine glasses.

'I should also imagine Don Dealy is the sort of person who uses people,' Issy said slowly.

'To get where he's got you have to be ruthless.'

'All the same, Lucinda's attitude towards me was a bit over the top.'

'There was talk of her brother having a bit of a thing going for your mother.'

'Finlay?'

'You've heard of him?'

'Isn't Lucinda's Arts Festival dedicated to his memory?'

'That's right.'

'And he knew my mother?'

'I think they were all part of the same set. You'll have to ask Lucinda for the details.'

'I doubt I'll get another invite. She cold-shouldered me. Shame, really,' Issy mused.

'Why's that?'

'I don't know. There was something about her I quite liked. Does that make sense?'

'Not much,' Ed replied, smiling into her eyes, 'but it shows what a generous person you really are if you can say that about someone who wasn't very welcoming.'

It may have been the wine making her feel drowsy, thought Issy, or the low lighting softening his features, but Ed was beginning to look half attractive away from the harsh strip lighting of the station coffee bar.

'Where did you get that jumper?' she asked.

'What's wrong with it?' Ed looked at down at the orange creation he was wearing.

'It's a bit vibrant.'

'If you must know, it was a present from my mother.'

'Hey,' Issy did her best to correct her gaffe. 'I don't want to upset her.'

'What's wrong with it?'

'Nothing. It's fine, really it is.'

'No it isn't,' Ed responded. 'It's awful. Mum went to knitting classes in the winter and this was her first attempt. I promised I'd wear it from time to time, but it doesn't fit very well and it's a bit itchy. To be honest, I'm scared to go out in public. People might mistake it for a high-visibility vest. It could get me into all sorts of trouble.'

They both burst out laughing.

'Please don't tell your mother what I said,' Issy implored.

'If I don't, you owe me one.'

Issy decided this had to be her last glass of wine. It was too tricky, fancying a man wearing a vibrant orange jumper; a man she was still not sure she totally trusted.

'How did you leave things with Don?' Ed asked.

'There was a vague invitation to 'do this again sometime', but Lucinda was hovering so I'm not holding my breath.'

'If anything comes of it, want me to join you for moral support?'

'I can look after myself,' Issy insisted. 'Anyway, Don might recognise you and it could ruin things.'

'Our paths have never crossed.'

'It's not worth the risk.' Issy shook her head.

'Have it your own way then,' Ed replied. 'Has there been any more response to your advert?'

'I've had a letter from a Roger Street in Australia.'

Ed whistled under his breath. 'So he's crawled out of the woodwork?'

'You know him?'

'According to my research, he was another one who was part of the Swallow House set.'

There had actually been a pencilled comment in the margin of Jonathan's notes. Roger Street had been heavily implicated in the Swallow House affair, but had taken off to Spain before charges could be levelled against him.

'He put me in touch with his brother. Harry Willetts?' Issy said before Ed could decide whether or not to pass on that piece of information.

'I didn't know he had a brother.'

'Is there any reason why you should?'

'I suppose not really. What did he have to say for himself?'

'We have a date for tomorrow night.'

'It's no good my offering to come with you tomorrow night either, is it?'

'None at all,' Issy insisted.

'I thought we were a team.'

'You're working on the case files. Can I see them?'

Ed coughed and spilt some wine.

'Went down the wrong way,' he apologised.

He leapt up and retrieved a cloth from the kitchen area. Coming back, he wiped the table, then went back for some kitchen towel to dry it.

'There, that's better. Now, where were we?'

'I was asking about your case files.'

'I don't have any.'

'What sort of partnership is that?' Issy's face pinkened in annoyance.

'I've sort of jotted down relevant notes from the online records.'

'I could have done that,' Issy pointed out.

'I know,' Ed acknowledged, not looking in the least abashed by the putdown, 'but you still need me on your side.'

'Why?'

'When things start getting down and dirty, I'm your man.'

'Are things likely to get down and dirty?' Issy enquired.

'You never know when you start raking up the past. Someone's always got something to hide.'

Ed's faint Yorkshire accent was comforting, making it difficult to believe he could be lying; but Issy still suspected he was holding out on her.

She finished her wine.

'No more.' She put a hand over her glass. 'I have to get back. They close the hostel doors at eleven and I don't want to have to rouse the porter.'

'I'll call a cab.' Ed picked up the telephone. 'Where are you meeting Harry tomorrow night?'

'Why do you want to know?'

'Just a precaution.'

'In case I disappear and am never heard of again?'

'Stranger things have happened.'

'Ollie's, it's a wine bar.'

The goodbye touch of Ed's lips on

her cheek had felt like a branding iron. Issy leaned back in the seat of her cab. Her head was in a whirl.

So far her advert had provided four contacts: Ed Stanwood, Don Dealy, Roger Street and Harry Willetts. Four very different men; and all of them, she suspected, had something to hide.

6

'Issy's got a thing going with Ed Stanwood. They've been seen together.'

'Right.' Harry stifled a yawn and waited for more. He hadn't been expecting Roger Street to log on this early. The man was clearly no respecter of international time zones.

'Ed Stanwood? Jonathan Jackson's nephew?' Roger now sounded impatient.

'Who is Jonathan Jackson?' Harry scratched the back of his head and wished he'd got to bed earlier last night.

'Shape up, Harry,' Roger barked at him. 'There are other actors for the job.'

Harry yawned again. 'It's only five in the morning here.'

'Well, it isn't here. You'd better be on better form tonight.'

'Chill,' Harry reassured him.

Roger frowned at the computer

screen. 'Are you listening to me? Your eyes are closed.'

Harry did his best to sit up straight.

'This isn't just any female, this is Issy Dillaine and she is Amy Grant's daughter.'

'The girl you stitched up.'

'Not at all, and you'd be well advised to keep remarks like that to yourself.' Roger's eyes narrowed to slits.

'Only joking,' Harry backtracked.

'Obviously we don't share the same sense of humour.' Roger held up a hand to stall Harry. 'We're wandering off the point. You need to know about Ed Stanwood. He's an investigative journalist.'

Harry paused in drinking his black coffee.

'Hey, wasn't he the one who exposed that offshore financial scandal? Some oligarch was creaming off millions. Brilliant stuff. Why's he mixed up with Issy?'

'Aren't you listening? I told you, his uncle is Jonathan Jackson. He was a junior on the team for the prosecution.'

'Does Issy know this?'

'I doubt it, but keep the information under your hat unless you absolutely have to use it.'

'To get me out of trouble, you mean?'

'Exactly.'

'What do you want me to do with Issy?'

'I want you to find out if her mother left her anything.'

'Like what?'

'Private papers, mementoes, a diary . . . ?'

'A written record of her life?'

'That sort of thing.'

'I'll see what I can do,' Harry said in a bored voice. He was beginning to wonder if the whole thing wasn't too much effort.

'Now, the backstory is: I'm the only member of your family who's kept in touch with you. You've fallen out with the rest of them because they do not understand your artistic ambitions.'

'Hardly that artistic. I've only had one part in a soap opera and they killed off my character after a measly two months,' Harry grumbled.

'That's why I picked you. There's not the faintest chance Issy will have seen you in anything significant.'

'Thanks a bunch.'

'This is not the time for wounded pride. You're being paid, well paid, to do a job, so it's vital you get your act together.'

'What's the relationship between us?'

'We have different fathers. That should be enough detail. I don't think Issy will be that interested. Her agenda will be focused on her mother. I also want you to find out exactly what she is looking for and how far she's got with her investigations. She'll probably be quite a tough cookie, so don't push it.'

'Do you have a picture of Issy?'

'No, I don't.'

'How am I going to recognise her?'

'Where are you meeting up?'

'Ollie's, it's a wine bar.'

'Then be outside on time and look for a girl on her own. And take a red rose.'

'You're kidding me.'

'It'll look good. Believe me. Now, I've booked two rooms in a Bayswater hotel. You can move in tomorrow.'

'Two rooms?'

'You'll have to stay there too.'

'Why?'

'I need you on hand to help set up a Skype link. I want to meet her face to face.'

'Expenses?' Harry asked.

'Within reason. I'll be keeping tabs on the bill.'

'If she's as feisty as you say she is may not want to move into a hotel.'

'Where is she staying now?'

'In a hostel.'

'She'll have to go somewhere when her week's up, and I don't think she has anyone in London she can stay with. I don't foresee any problems. You are still up for it? I don't want you letting me down at the last moment. I've a lot riding on this one.'

'I'll give it a try.'

'I need more than that. I need your

full commitment, Harry. If you want out, I need to know now.'

'I've said I'll do it and I will,' Harry insisted. 'I won't go back on my word.'

'See you don't.'

'Anything else?' Harry asked.

'You're to report back to me on a daily basis. That way I can keep tabs on things.'

'Got it.'

Harry made sure he had switched off before allowing a sly smile to cross his face. If there was any money to be made out of this one he intended to get a slice of the action. If Roger Street was interested in Issy Dillaine then other people would be too; people who would be prepared to pay. Humming to himself, Harry went looking for something suitable to wear.

* * *

Ollie's was tucked away down a quiet side street on the site of an old

72

marketplace. A bitter wind whipped round the corner. Harry was fuming. He was used to arriving late and having his date waiting for him, not the other way round. He did not like standing on the pavement, clutching a wilting red rose and being stood up in the freezing cold.

A bunch of girls huddled together for warmth giggled at him.

'On your own?' one of them teased. 'You can always join us. We'll show you a good time.'

Harry's cheeks reddened as they blew kisses then made their way inside. He was giving it five more minutes, then he was off. The job wasn't worth it.

One or two flakes of snow began to drift down from the sky and land gently on the pavement. They sparkled, catching the light from an ornate street lamp left over from the market days but Harry was in no mood for snowflakes.

'Right, that's it,' he decided and

turned in the direction of the Underground, oblivious to the sound of approaching tyres on the wet cobblestones.

He heard a breathless voice behind him as he strode towards the tube station. 'Are you Harry Willetts? I'm Issy Dillaine.'

He spun round.

'You're late and I don't like being kept waiting,' he snapped before he remembered Roger's advice. He thrust the rose at the blonde-haired girl standing on the pavement.

Neither of them moved as the taxi drove off.

'This is for you.'

Issy ignored the gesture.

'I wouldn't have been late if you'd given me decent directions,' she protested. 'The taxi driver didn't know where Ollie's was and neither did I. We've been driving round for half an hour.'

'He should have used satnav,' Harry replied.

'You didn't give me the postcode.'

Snow was now falling steadily around them. In the light from the tube station Harry could see Issy's eyelashes were damp from a coating of wet snow. She was a knockout, he thought. He liked her style too. She didn't take any lip.

'Shall we go inside?' he suggested, his good humour restored. Perhaps this evening wasn't going to be a total waste of time after all. He tossed the damp rose into a wastepaper bin. 'It was past its best,' he explained. 'Look,' he inspected the sky, 'I even arranged for it to snow to make you feel at home. It does snow in your part of the world?' he asked. 'Or is it rain you get by the bucketload?'

Issy's eyes didn't soften. Harry took a deep breath. She was proving to be hard work.

'I apologise for being a grouch.' He feigned a sneeze. 'But I shall blame you if I come down with double pneumonia because you've made me stand out here while you're making up your mind if you like the look of me.' Harry paused. 'Do we still have a date?'

'You're too fresh by half.'

'Which is more than can be said for that rose. Come on. Let's get inside before we freeze to the ground. We can argue later.'

Harry linked his arms through Issy's and guided her away from the underground entrance and into the dark warmth of the wine bar.

'The lady's coat is wet. Can you hang it up somewhere to dry?'

He handed it over, took off his own coat and, without a second glance at the attendant, ushered Issy towards the only vacant table.

'Be back in a minute,' he promised. 'Sit down and make yourself comfortable.'

Issy looked round the darkened interior of the busy bar. It wouldn't have been her first choice of venue for a business discussion, but she felt safe here. Bearing in mind Ed's concern, she'd told a roommate at the hostel where she was going and that she hoped to be back by eleven. Easing out the tension at the back of her neck, she closed her eyes.

'Here we are.'

Harry was back with a bottle of white wine in an ice bucket and two glasses.

'How did you manage to get served so quickly?'

'If you wave a note at the barman it works. I told him to keep the change. What's that you've got there?' Harry asked as she withdrew a sheet of paper from her handbag.

'Your brother's letter.'

'Down to business already, is it?'

'That is why we're here,' she reminded him.

'How about we first drink a toast?' He handed a glass to Issy. 'What shall we drink to?'

'Success?' Issy suggested.

Harry's eyes met hers as they chinked glasses.

'Success it is,' he agreed with a confident smile.

7

Ed looked at the jug of fresh orange juice he had been sharing with his uncle and wished it was hot chocolate. It was cold on the terrace of the wharfside complex apartment; but, after years of working in stuffy courtrooms, Jonathan had turned into a fresh-air freak and worked outside whenever he could, no matter the temperature. His diet too had had a makeover, which explained the jug of fresh-squeezed orange.

'You don't mind sitting outside, do you?' he asked his nephew. 'There's a lovely view of the marina.'

Glad he'd thought to wear a warm shirt under his fleece, Ed assured Jonathan he was absolutely fine.

'Looks like we could be in for more snow later,' Jonathan said, with a trace of anticipation in his voice.

'We haven't finished with the last lot

yet,' Ed replied, his breath misting the air.

Although bad weather made little impact on this part of London, several of the moored craft in the marina still showed a light dusting of snow on their canvas.

'Any news?' Jonathan changed the subject.

'Not a lot,' Ed conceded. 'I'm beginning to wonder if the whole thing isn't a waste of time.'

'You're not losing heart, are you?' An anxious frown wrinkled Jonathan's brow.

'I'm not getting anywhere with Issy. She's been down to see Don Dealy and met up with Harry Willetts, but she wouldn't let me go with her either time and I'm left kicking my heels feeling like the spare man at a wedding.'

'Harry Willetts, is he the half-brother no one's heard of?' Jonathan asked.

'Yes. Roger arranged for Issy to meet up with him in a wine bar and the next thing I know she's moved out of the hostel and into a hotel, all at Roger's expense.'

'Now, that is interesting.' Jonathan's eyes lit up.

'Not to me, it isn't.'

'Roger Street never does anything without good reason. He wants Issy in his clutches.'

'Why doesn't he fly over from Australia and do his own dirty work then?' Ed grumbled.

'He might feel things are a bit too hot for him here.'

'After all this time?'

'Exactly. There's no reason for him not to come, so why doesn't he?' Jonathan reasoned.

'Pressure of work?'

'I'm more than ever convinced he knows more about what went on than he's saying.'

'Is that your legal opinion or a gut feeling?'

Jonathan leaned forward. 'Where did Roger get the money from to set up his own business?'

'I don't know.' Ed hazarded a guess: 'Networking? From what you tell me he sounds a pretty sociable guy.'

'When he and Amy were hanging around together he was no more than an ambitious office boy.'

'Office boys do rise through the ranks.'

'Maybe, but his rise was pretty meteoric by anyone's standards. First he disappears off to Spain, leaving Amy in the lurch.'

'That wasn't good,' Ed agreed.

'The next time anyone hears from him, he's in Australia living the high life. He travels a lot in Asia, but he never comes back here; which I find strange.' Jonathan narrowed his eyes.

'What about his family?' Ed asked.

'That's another thing. He doesn't have a past.'

'Everyone's got a past.'

'Like so much else about him, Roger didn't leave any fingerprints.'

'So you don't believe the story of this brother?'

'I don't,' Jonathan said, 'and I want to know what Roger is up to.'

'One thing is for certain,' Ed pointed out, 'Amy made nothing out of the affair.' He sipped his juice.

'That's why I would like to clear her name.'

'Can you tell me anything more about her, fill me in a bit on her background?'

Jonathan pondered for a moment before replying.

'She was brought up in Surrey. By all accounts she seems to have had a very ordinary childhood. She kicked over the traces a bit in her teens, nothing too serious, but eventually she seems to have settled down and applied to be a ground hostess with an airline. Apparently she spoke fluent Italian, and with her looks she was perfect for the job. That's how she met Roger Street. The story goes that his boss asked Amy to mail a letter to his office for him. This was in the days before email, you understand. Anyway, Amy forgot about it, and when she found it in the bottom of her handbag she panicked and decided to deliver it personally. For some reason Roger was hanging round the post room that day and took charge of it, and that's how they got together.'

'This letter?'

'It was quite straightforward, something to do with a rescheduled interview. There were no leads there. Like so much else in this affair it came to nothing.'

'If Roger was involved with the perpetrators of this scam, how did they meet?'

'I don't know how they linked up, but he was suspected of bringing some guests along to one of Don's parties. Amy was amongst their number. I think he originally ingratiated himself with Lucinda or that brother of hers. It's all rather vague.'

'You mentioned,' Ed chose his words carefully, 'that Amy was a beautiful girl?'

'I only saw her in the flesh once; but yes, she was beautiful.' Jonathan gave his nephew a man-of-the-world look. 'From that question, I infer the daughter is very like her mother?'

'Issy's beautiful all right.' Ed flushed under his uncle's scrutiny. 'She's also spunky and doesn't suffer fools gladly, so if you do meet her I'd watch your step.'

There was a twinkle in Jonathan's eye as he said, 'She sounds exactly the sort of girl for you.'

'What do you want me to do now?' Ed ignored his uncle's comment.

'I'm not sure. Issy's been to see Don Dealy? Do you know what happened at this meeting?'

'His wife Lucinda Whitby was a bit frosty.'

'That I find surprising. Lucinda likes young people.'

'Perhaps Don was another one who was in love with Amy.'

'I don't think so. He was married to Lucinda, and for all his shortcomings theirs is a rock-solid relationship. There's never been the slightest whiff of a scandal of that nature.' Jonathan paused. 'Do you think you could arrange an interview with him?'

'The entertainment industry isn't really my scene, especially not his sort of stuff.' Ed wrinkled his nose, remembering his heated exchange of views with Issy on the subject. 'Besides, even if I cobbled together an excuse to interview him, how on earth could I suddenly introduce the subject of Amy Grant? He'd be bound to smell a rat.'

'What about his wife?' Jonathan suggested.

'Lucinda?' Ed felt a tingle of excitement down his spine. 'Now, there we could have a hit. She's always on the look out for publicity for her youth workshop.'

'Then give it a go.'

'What about Harry Willetts?' Ed asked. 'The so-called brother?'

'I don't know what he and Roger are up to, but I suppose as long as Issy is resident in a respectable hotel she shouldn't come to any harm. Is that your telephone or mine?' Jonathan asked as a ringtone interrupted them.

'It's a text from Issy,' Ed replied. 'She wants to meet up.'

'Then, dear boy, I suggest you finish your orange juice and take the lady up on her invitation. From what you've told me, it doesn't do to keep her waiting.'

★ ★ ★

Issy's hotel was tucked away in a quiet corner of Bayswater. At reception, Ed was informed that Ms Dillaine was in the coffee lounge. He took a few moments to check her out, unobserved, through the glass of the door.

She was wearing a shocking pink sweater and black leggings, and minimal make-up. Her blonde hair shone with health. Some businessmen enjoying a late-afternoon coffee at an adjacent table cast envious glances in Ed's direction as he pushed open the door and strode towards her.

'Hi.' She smiled at him, a dimple denting her cheek. 'How're things?'

He sat down opposite her.

'I was fine until I saw your sweater,' he said.

'What's wrong with it?'

'It's a bit pink,' he joked, 'and to think you made me abandon my high-visibility orange one.'

When she laughed he tried not to notice how the deep blue of her eyes reminded him of a summer sea. He could totally understand Jonathan's manly pangs of emotion for her mother.

'But what's been happening to you? I thought you were staying at the hostel.'

'Developments.' She was still smiling as she added, 'My week was up, and when Harry suggested we move here I agreed.'

'At Roger Street's expense?' Ed had difficulty containing his disbelief after Issy told him the rest of the story.

'I'm actually paying my own bill.' Ed watched the warmth leave Issy's eyes.

'Not that it's any business of yours,' she added.

'I just think you don't want to owe Roger any favours.'

'I don't, and if you must know, another reason we moved here was because he wanted to set up a Skype link so we could communicate visually.'

'And have you?'

'Not yet.' Issy tossed back her head as if challenging him to make something of it. Ed opened his mouth but wasn't given the chance to speak. 'I don't need any lectures from you.' Her eyes flashed dangerously.

'I haven't given you one,' Ed protested.

'But you were about to. I could see it in your face. Ed, I know what I'm doing, so I suggest you stick to your part of the deal and I'll stick to mine.'

Ed wasn't too sure what his part of the deal was, and whether or not Issy realised what she could be getting into, but he didn't want to lose her trust or her friendship.

'OK.' He did his best to smooth things over. 'Am I allowed to ask about Harry?'

'He's out at the moment. I'll introduce you when he gets back.'

'What does he do?'

'He said his background was farming, but he didn't strike me as a country boy.' Issy wrinkled her nose. 'He was too at home in the wine bar.'

'Livestock? Arable?'

'The farm? He didn't talk about it much.'

'I bet,' Ed couldn't help replying.

'What's that remark supposed to mean?'

'Nothing,' Ed said quickly, anxious to prevent another scene. 'How long is he staying here?'

'I don't know,' Issy admitted.

'Does he know about us?'

'I haven't told him, but we don't have anything to hide, do we?'

'Not really; only I thought I was working undercover.'

'You're starting to sound like a spy.

You're not one, are you?' she asked after a short pause.

'Course I'm not.' Ed hoped his reaction hadn't been too swift.

'There's no need to look so guilty, I'm only teasing.'

Ed flushed a dull red. Issy was proving more of a handful than many of his previous assignments.

'If you didn't talk about farming, what did you talk about?'

'Harry wanted to know if my mother left me any paperwork, or written records of what happened at Swallow House.'

'And did she?' Ed asked.

'No, but don't you think it was an odd question?'

'Issy?'

She turned as someone called her name.

'Harry.' She waved him over. Harry glanced across to where Ed was sitting.

'Meet Ed Stanwood. Ed, this is Harry.'

The two men shook hands.

'Sit down and tell us what you've been up to,' Issy invited.

'Nothing very much,' Harry replied, his eyes never leaving Ed's face.

'Have we met before?' Ed asked, unnerved by Harry's scrutiny.

'I don't think so,' Harry said, then clicked his fingers. 'Hold on, you're that Ed Stanwood, aren't you? The reporter. What's your game?' Harry demanded.

'Ed and I met as a result of my advert,' Issy intervened.

'Are you hoping to make megabucks out of Issy's story?'

'That's not my style.'

'What is with you two? Stop snarling at each other.' Issy looked from Ed to Harry.

'The *mother-I-never-knew* stuff? *How my heart was broken by what I found out?*' Harry's lip curled in disgust. 'That's sick.'

'Harry,' Issy objected.

'It's no sicker than pretending to be what I'm not.'

'Ed, that's enough.' Issy now turned to face him.

He shook her hand off his arm. 'You're no more a pig farmer than I am.'

'It wasn't pigs,' Harry objected.

'It wasn't anything. You're a bit-part actor. You were in that crummy soap that got pulled from the schedules, weren't you? You didn't last past the second episode. Is this your latest part? Pretending to be Roger Street's brother?'

Their raised voices were now drawing interested looks from the neighbouring businessmen.

'Is this true?' Issy demanded. 'Are you really an actor?'

'There's is no point in denying it,' Harry admitted. 'I'm no relation to Roger Street.'

'And he asked you to find out all you could about Issy and report back to him?' Ed pursued his line of questioning.

'Something along those lines.'

'Then I think you'd better leave.' Issy's voice was ice-cold.

'I'll go when I'm ready.' Harry leaned back in his armchair, looking like a cat faced with a dish of cream. 'I haven't broken any law. So, Ed,' he crossed his arms, 'you've found me out.' He paused. 'While we're exchanging confidences, why don't you return the favour?'

'What do you mean?' Ed asked with a wary look.

'You know exactly what I mean, Ed Stanwood; but I'm not sure Issy does, do you?'

Harry turned his attention in her direction. Issy looked perplexed.

'Tell Issy, Ed, why don't you?'

'Tell her what?' Ed's jaw tightened.

'You mean you're not who you say you are either?' Issy had now turned pale.

'He's who he says he is all right,' Harry acknowledged, 'but I bet he left out the best bit. I bet he didn't tell you about his uncle.'

'You mentioned your uncle the day we met.' Issy was looking full-on at Ed. 'Something to do with him making you late?'

'They were probably cooking up a nice little story,' Harry answered for Ed.

'What's so special about Ed's uncle?'

'His name is Jonathan Jackson.'

'Jonathan Jackson?' Issy repeated in a confused voice.

'Shall I tell her who he is, or would you like to do the honours?' Harry asked. When Ed didn't speak, he continued, 'It looks like it's up to me, then. Jonathan Jackson, QC retired, was part of the prosecution team on the Swallow House case. They did their best to get Amy convicted.'

8

'You blew his cover?' Roger's face was a mask of barely concealed fury.

'What else was I supposed to do?' Harry looked equally rattled. 'I was thinking on my feet.'

'Where's Issy now?' Roger demanded.

'Booking out.'

'Then stop her.'

'How?'

'Get her to change her mind. You don't have any idea where Ed's gone?'

'None at all. Issy stormed out of the coffee lounge and he stormed after her. I felt such a fool sitting there with everyone looking at me.'

'It's no more than you deserve. Now get going before Issy disappears too.' Roger cut the video link.

Harry tapped on Issy's door. 'Hi, Issy, it's me. Can we talk?'

He stepped back swiftly as Issy

yanked open the door.

'I have absolutely nothing to say to you.'

'Hear me out,' Harry pleaded.

'I'm busy packing.'

'Five minutes, no more?'

'What do you want?' Issy relented.

'Can I come in?'

'No.' She crossed her arms in a gesture of confrontation. 'You can say your bit in the corridor.'

Casting a nervous glance over his shoulder, Harry said, 'I've been talking to Roger and he really wants to keep in touch with you. So do I,' Harry added.

'You lied to me. Ed lied to me. I expect Don Dealy lied as well. Doesn't anyone in this country tell the truth?'

'That's not fair,' Harry protested. 'All right, maybe I'm not Roger's brother, but we didn't do anything wrong.'

Issy's mouth dropped open.

'Do neither of you have any concept of the truth?'

'Roger asked me to keep an eye on you. Anyway, you started it with your advert. Roger thought if I pretended to be his brother it would make things,' Harry ran a hand through his hair, 'more respectable?'

'I haven't a clue what you're talking about.'

Harry gritted his teeth. 'You don't make things easy for a guy, do you?'

'I don't have to.'

'If I'd approached you as a total stranger, you would have had every reason to be wary of me.'

'Harry, you're a conman.' Issy pushed him away as he began to invade her personal space.

'I'm an actor. If you want an example of a conman, then look no further than Ed Stanwood. He really did sell you a line.'

'Can we please not talk about him?' Issy asked through tightened lips.

'Sure, anything you say.' Harry pressed home his advantage. 'I'm staying on, and I'd really like it if you did the same. We could link up with Roger later and talk things through.

Anyway, why do you want to go traipsing around the streets looking for somewhere to stay when you've got a perfectly good room here? It's cold out there and there's more snow on the way.'

Issy hesitated.

'Look, the whole idea of coming over here was to find out about your mother, right?'

'Yes.'

'Roger's a good lead. He knew her intimately and he's prepared to talk to you.'

Issy chewed her lower lip, then nodded reluctantly.

'All right; but no more lies?'

'Hand on heart,' Harry promised. 'Now, as we didn't get any tea and I missed out on lunch, how about something to eat?'

Issy had been too upset to eat as well, and now her nerves were calming down she realised she too was hungry.

'I'll get my coat and bag. Wait there.'

She emerged a few minutes later and

locked her door.

'There's a pizza bar down the street.' Harry pressed the lift button. 'I know you said we weren't to talk about Ed,' he began as the lift arrived and they got in, 'but where's he gone?'

The tough look was back on Issy's face. 'I don't know, but he won't be coming round here again.'

'Now, that is good news.'

Ignoring Harry's confident smile Issy strode towards the reception desk.

'There was a telephone call for you, Ms Dillaine,' the receptionist smiled.

'Who was it from?' Issy asked.

'Don Dealy?' The receptionist raised her eyebrows. 'Did I get the name right? Is that *the* Don Dealy?'

'What was the message?'

'He wondered if you were free this weekend.'

'You order up two pizzas,' Issy instructed Harry who was hovering behind her. 'I need to return Don's call.'

'He's not trying to recruit you for

that talent show of his, is he?' Harry asked. 'Do you think he'd be interested in a resting actor? If so, I'm available.'

'I'll see you in five minutes,' Issy informed him in a firm voice, and gave him a shove towards the revolving door.

'Don?' Issy was pleased to hear his warm voice answer her call.

'Darling, hello, how are you?'

'I'm fine.'

'I had a bit of trouble tracking you down. I thought you were still at the hostel. They wouldn't tell me where you were to begin with. I'm ashamed to say I played the celebrity card. It's not something I do very often, but I couldn't think how else to find you.'

'Sorry, Don,' Issy apologised. 'I should have let you know I'd moved out.'

'No matter. As long as we're still on speaking terms, I'm sorry your last visit was cut short. The thing is . . . ' Don cleared his throat. 'Lucinda's off somewhere planning one of her fundraisers. I'm not going with her so I wondered if we could have that little chat I promised you?'

'That would be lovely.' Issy's voice betrayed her uncertainty.

Don picked up on her reluctance to commit. 'I sense a *but* coming on.'

'Have you ever lied to me?' Issy demanded.

'That's an extraordinary question.' Don sounded surprised. 'What sparked it off?'

'I've had two other responses to my advert and both of them were economical with the truth.'

'I can assure you, Issy, I am exactly who I say I am. You need have no worries on that score. You can check up on me if you like. I could give you my agent's number.'

'I'm sorry, Don,' Issy replied, embarrassed by her outburst. 'I didn't mean to sound rude, only I've had it up to here with phonies.'

'There's no need to apologise. These things happen. In my time I've met my fair share of impostors. Now, I can't wait to see you again. I'm also a very good cook, so please say you'll visit. You'll break my heart if you don't.'

'I'd love to.' Issy laughed.

'Excellent. You can sleep over in the nursery if you want to. You liked that room, didn't you?'

Issy felt a warm feeling in the pit of her stomach as she remembered the few quiet moments she had enjoyed in the room before Don and Lucinda burst in on the scene.

'It was how I imagined a perfect nursery would be,' she admitted, recalling the feeling that someone was watching over her as she rocked back and forth on the horse.

'Then it's yours for the weekend.'

Issy longed to ask why a couple with no children had furnished a room with such love and care, but now was not the time for such an intensely personal question.

It was only as she finished the call that Issy realised Don hadn't actually answered her question about whether or not he had told her an untruth.

'I'll have your bill ready shortly,' the receptionist said as Issy handed in her key.

'I've changed my mind,' she replied, 'if that's all right with you? I'd like to stay on.'

'No problem. I couldn't help overhearing your conversation. I wish I were spending the weekend with Don Dealy. He's so charismatic isn't he? You know, the man you love to hate? He has such presence on the screen, and the things he comes out with . . . You can't help laughing even if at times he can be a bit hurtful.'

'I've never seen him on television.'

'He's not to everybody's taste, I suppose. Actually, I know I shouldn't say this — what with Don being, well, friendly with you — but,' the receptionist leaned forward, 'his name's not really Don Dealy.'

'Isn't it?'

'One of our guests was at school with him. He told me he's really called

Donald Sidebottom.'

'No wonder he changed it.' Issy joined in her laughter.

'And he won't see fifty-five again.'

The manager poked his head out of the back office and beckoned the receptionist over.

'Was there anything else, madam?' She stopped gossiping and, straightening up, assumed a bright, professional voice.

'What? Oh no, thank you very much,' Issy replied.

'Then we'll keep the room on for you.'

The receptionist disappeared into the back office. Forgetting all about her pizza date with Harry, Issy headed towards the lift; glad that if Don was guilty of telling little white lies, it was only in the name of publicity.

9

Ed eased his tie away from his collar and grimaced. Why did everyone of his uncle's generation insist on meeting in places that maintained a dress code? He was used to working in an environment where just getting through the day unscathed was a challenged. No one gave a toot what you wore.

He glanced again at his watch. Lucinda Whitby was forty minutes late and the waiter on reception was beginning to cast questioning looks in his direction.

When he had contacted her, he hadn't expected her to be quite so amenable to his approach. 'Darling,' she'd gushed, 'I'd love to be inter-viewed by you. I adore your stuff, so cutting-edge.'

Ed had made a self-deprecating noise at the back of his throat.

'That's very kind of you, Miss Whitby.'

'Lucinda will do fine. And there's absolutely no need for you to travel out to the country: I've business meetings scheduled in town later this week. Shall we say Friday afternoon? I can be with you about four o'clock if that child of a wardrobe mistress doesn't keep me. Honestly, how anyone that young can hold down such a responsible job, I do not know. I've got a small but significant part in a costume drama,' she added. 'I'm afraid the days are gone when I could play the young lead. Now I have to make do with the matronly parts.'

Before Ed had been given the chance to explain why he wanted to talk to Lucinda, she had rung off.

It was another cold day. Charcoal clouds scudded across a leaden sky, reflecting Ed's mood.

'Our cover's blown,' he had informed his uncle, 'and Issy never wants to see me again.'

He went on to explain about Harry and all that had happened at the hotel.

'It was only to be expected, I suppose,' had been Jonathan's reply. 'No matter. How did you get on with her before the bust-up?'

'I'm not sure how to answer that,' Ed admitted.

'You liked her, didn't you?'

'Yes, I did. What you see is what you get with Issy.'

'Maybe those Irish relations didn't do such a bad job.'

'I have fixed a date to meet up with Lucinda Whitby, Don's wife, if you still want to go ahead with your amateur sleuthing,' Ed had added.

'I'll understand if you want out,' Jonathan said.

'I don't,' Ed admitted.

'I didn't think you were all that enthusiastic in the beginning. What's changed your mind?'

Ed wasn't sure. Having Harry reveal his uncle's past in such a dramatic way had not been the high experience of a lifetime, and Issy's public declaration that he was the human equivalent of pond life wasn't much better, but her words had ignited an emotion inside him. He could feel her sense of betrayal, wanted to make things up to her, and the only way he could do that was to prove Amy's innocence.

He was glad Jonathan had never met Issy, otherwise he might have formed his own conclusions concerning Ed's change of heart. As it was, he did his best to convince his uncle that his investigative interest could contain the nucleus of a newsworthy story.

Ed fidgeted in his seat. It was now a quarter to five: way past the time he had agreed to meet up with Lucinda. He couldn't eke out his beer any longer. He finished his drink and stood up.

The waiter approached.

'Would it be possible to leave a message for Lucinda Whitby?' Ed asked.

'Certainly, sir, but wouldn't you

prefer to give it to her yourself?'

'She seems to have been delayed.'

'Her lunch has rather overrun,' the waiter agreed. 'I could have a discreet word in her ear. I know the waiting staff are eager to lay the table up for dinner.'

'You mean she's been here all the time?' Ed stifled his irritation.

'In the restaurant, sir. I thought you knew.'

'Did anyone tell her I'd arrived?'

'Of that I can't be sure. Do you have a card?'

Ed passed one over.

'If you'd care to wait here, I'll personally pass on your message.'

It was another fifteen minutes before Ed heard a flurry in the doorway and an extremely refreshed Lucinda greeted him.

'I am so sorry,' she gushed. 'The girls kept me talking about the old times. You know what it's like. No,' she beamed at him, 'I don't suppose you do. You're not an old girl, are you?' She detained another passing waiter with a wave of her be-ringed hand. 'May we have some coffee please, and perhaps a plate of those delicious chocolate mints? Now, where shall we sit?'

Choosing one of the sofas, Lucinda spread out and gestured Ed to an adjacent seat.

'We haven't met before, have we? I'm sure I would have remembered such a handsome young man.'

Lucinda had what could kindly be described as a character face. Little was known of her background. Ed had tried to find out as much as he could but her parentage was shrouded in mystery, as was her exact age.

She had exploded onto the scene as an ingénue, after her debut film acquired cult status. From then on her star had risen. Ed strongly suspected she had invented what was known of her past, and that very little of it was true.

Her career had dipped just as Don's had started to rise, and now he was the major player in the marriage. They had been together for many years, and theirs was one of the most solid unions in an industry not renowned for the longevity of its liaisons. They were both passionate about their youth programme and the arts festival they staged every summer; though the programme had suffered a blip after the Swallow House Summer (as the press had dubbed it), it had stayed the course and was now a regular fixture on the arts circuit.

'What was it exactly you wanted to interview me about?' Lucinda asked, fixing her deep blue eyes on Ed.

'Amy Grant.'

Ed decided to come right out with it after having wasted a whole afternoon sitting around twiddling his thumbs.

'I see,' was Lucinda's cool response.

Ed knew she was far too professional to betray her true feelings about Amy to someone she did not know.

'Is this by any chance to do with that young lady who visited Don recently?'

'Issy Dillaine?'

111

'Yes, that was her name.'

Ed decided to play dumb.

'How did you meet up with her after all this time?'

'Don answered an advert she placed in the newspaper. I discouraged him, but he didn't take my advice. Amy Grant was Issy's mother. I think the poor child entertained some ridiculous notion that Amy and Don were close.'

'Were they?'

Lucinda raised an eyebrow.

'That is something you had better ask him yourself.'

Ed recognised her remark for the rebuff it was.

'Can we talk about the Swallow House summer party?'

'Which one?' Lucinda asked, a wary look in her eye.

'The one when Amy supposedly met her contacts.'

'I'd rather not go into all that again. I thought this interview was about my youth programme.'

'You scratch my back and I'll scratch

yours,' Ed replied. 'That's the way it works, isn't it?'

'Publicity for an exclusive?'

'Shall we say, a new slant on the story?'

A look of distaste crossed Lucinda's face. 'It was so long ago it would mean nothing to a modern generation.'

'I thought maybe I could get a fresh angle on what happened.'

'Regarding what exactly?'

'Credit card fraud was in its infancy.'

'And I'm not sure I want to be associated with it.'

'Amy was supposed to have been introduced to the perpetrators at your party.'

'I don't know anything about any fraud,' Lucinda insisted. 'The police interviewed me for hours. My nerves were in a dreadful state. Don had to take me away on holiday to recover. Everything that needs to be said on Amy Grant has already been said.'

Ed was saved from preventing Lucinda getting up off the sofa by the arrival of the coffee tray. While the waiter poured out the coffee Ed glanced through some notes he had prepared before their meeting.

Lucinda unwrapped the silver foil off one of the mints and nibbled it thoughtfully.

'I might be prepared to negotiate with you,' she announced as the waiter left their table.

'What's the deal?' Ed asked.

'I do need publicity for my youth programme. It's getting very difficult to obtain sponsorship, and when you're no longer the face of today promoters aren't that interested. There's only so much I can ask Don to do.'

Ed nodded. Lucinda was speaking his language.

'Don and I have no children.' Lucinda raised an eyebrow and waited for Ed to say something. When he didn't respond she went on, 'We've always had an affinity for young people and we like to encourage them, but it isn't easy raising money.'

'You want me to pull a few publicity strings for you?'

'You're a very forthright young man,' Lucinda acknowledged, 'but yes, I suppose that is what I'm saying.'

'What would I get in return?'

'You were looking for a new angle on an old story?' Lucinda took another bite of chocolate mint.

'Are you prepared to offer me a taster as an expression of goodwill?' Ed held his breath, fearing he may have gone too far.

'You want to know what happened between Don and Amy Grant?'

Ed cleared his throat. 'I do.'

'Absolutely nothing happened between them.'

Ed bit down his disappointment. For someone who professed to be ignorant of what had gone on, Lucinda was adamant on that one.

'Do you think Amy was innocent of the charges levelled against her?'

'That's an old favourite,' Lucinda acknowledged, 'when there's nothing else on the news front. A pretty young girl accused of a crime she didn't commit always makes good cover for people to read over their Sunday breakfast. But nothing has ever come of any investigation.'

'So you've nothing new to tell me?'

Lucinda unwrapped her third mint.

'Have you heard of Roger Street?'

'Do you mind if I make notes?' Ed asked.

'I would prefer my remarks to be off the record.'

Ed held up his notebook. 'This will be the only record of our meeting. You have my word as a journalist.'

'That's not always the best recommendation,' Lucinda licked flakes of chocolate off her fingers, 'but I'll trust you in the hope that you won't let me down.'

'Roger Street?' Ed prompted.

'I didn't like him,' Lucinda pronounced.

'Why not?'

'Nothing I could put my finger on.

He was a perfect guest. He didn't behave badly. He was a good conversationalist and pleasant company.'

'How would you describe him in one word?' Ed asked.

Lucinda thought for a few moments.

'Oily,' she said.

Ed's pencil flew over the paper.

'Much of my background has been fabricated to suit the media and no one, not even eager young journalists, are going to get the truth out of me on that one.'

'Go on,' Ed urged, not wanting to stop the flow.

'Whilst my backstory was made up for purely professional purposes, I get the feeling Roger's re-invention was the product of a careful makeover.'

'Excuse me, madam, sir. May I pull the curtains?'

Ed jumped at the sound of the housekeeper's voice. While they had been talking the light had faded from the day, but neither of them had noticed.

The curtains swept across the picture window and the housekeeper adjusted the lamp behind Ed.

'See that we're not disturbed, would you?' Lucinda asked.

'Certainly, madam.' She removed the coffee tray. 'Can I get you anything to drink?'

'Later, perhaps. Leave the mints.'

'What about Amy?' Ed asked.

Lucinda attacked another mint.

'We could have been friends, but — well, there were reasons,' Lucinda paused, 'that I'm not prepared to go into now.'

'And you know nothing about the fraud?'

'Nothing at all.' Lucinda pursed her lips.

'Did you read up on the investigation?' Ed asked.

'Don kept the newspapers from me. They were saying the most scandalous things about us, things which he knew would distress me.' Lucinda finished the last mint on the plate, then extracted a white linen hankie from her bag and dabbed her eyes.

'Sorry,' she apologised. 'It was too much for me then and it's too much for me now, even after all these years.'

'I don't want to distress you, Lucinda.' Ed snapped shut his notebook. 'I've more than enough to be going on with and I won't forget our deal.'

'Bless you.' She delivered a watery smile. 'There's more, but not now.'

'I understand.'

'That was our last really big summer party. After that, our hearts weren't in it.' Lucinda sighed. 'But life goes on, although things were never quite the same again. Tell me, was Issy happy with her adopted parents?'

'I think so.'

'Then it all worked out for the best, didn't it?' Lucinda struggled to her feet. 'Now, if you'll excuse me?'

They shook hands, and Ed watched Lucinda teeter out of the lounge, his mind racing. He wondered what else Lucinda knew — and how much she wasn't telling him.

10

Issy perched on the end of her bed trying to make some notes. Ed, Roger and Harry had all deceived her. Don appeared genuine, but Issy was convinced he knew more than he was saying.

Her mobile signalled an incoming text from Harry.

I gave your pizza to the dog. C U around.

She sighed. She had completely forgotten her promise to join Harry for a pizza. He'd probably delete her reply unread but she sent an apology. She didn't feel like facing him now anyway, although her stomach reminded her she was still hungry.

'You're a popular girl today, Ms Dillaine,' the receptionist greeted her as she came out of the lift. 'I have another message for you. This one was hand-delivered by the porter from your hostel. It arrived there after you checked out.' She handed it over with a smile. 'Anything else I can do for you?'

'Do you think I could have a sandwich and some coffee in the bar please?' Issy asked.

The receptionist bustled away as Issy glanced at the envelope. It had originally been addressed to the box number allocated to her advert, and was typewritten on a business envelope and postmarked Sussex. Wandering into the bar, she sat down, immersed in deep thought. Did she want to carry on with her enquiries? So far, what she had found out hadn't brought her much joy. Perhaps she should return home and forget about her past.

The letter was from a warden of a residential home on the south coast and was a simple request for Issy to ring her. She put it to one side and sipped her coffee. It was warm and revived her flagging spirits. So too did the freshly-made sandwiches. Her head began to clear.

Finishing her snack, Issy dialled the telephone number displayed at the top of her latest letter.

'Hollies,' a brisk voice replied.

'I'd like to speak to the warden, please,' Issy said.

'May I know what it's in connection with?'

'My name is Issy Dillaine. Mrs Fay sent me a letter in reply to an advertisement I placed in a newspaper.'

'Just one moment, please.'

'Good evening, Ms Dillaine. Sally Fay speaking,' said another voice on the line. 'I understand you received my letter?'

'Yes.'

'I know your advert was placed a while ago, and I'm sorry we weren't in touch earlier; only our activities organiser left, and we haven't had a chance to appoint a new one. She's the member of staff who usually deals with matters of this nature.'

Issy hoped this call was not going to be yet another waste of time. She waited patiently for Sally Fay to continue.

'Does the name Bella Tucker mean anything to you?'

'Sorry, no, it doesn't,' Issy apologised, wondering where the conversation was leading.

'Mrs Tucker asked me to contact you. She likes to read the newspaper but she finds the print a bit small for her eyes.'

'And this Mrs Tucker was a friend of Amy Grant's?'

'She was more than that.' There was a pause before the warden announced: 'She was her mother.'

★ ★ ★

Issy hardly noticed the changing scenery as the train from Victoria sped through the countryside down towards the south coast.

When Harry had knocked on her bedroom door late last night she had pretended to be asleep, but in reality she had tossed and turned for hours until, unable to stay in bed any longer, she had got up early and taken a shower before being the first down to breakfast.

Her head was still reeling from the shock of discovering she had a grandmother. Mrs Fay hadn't given out much information over the telephone.

'We can talk better when you arrive,' she explained, 'but I can tell you Bella is very excited about this and looking forward to meeting you.'

'You don't know how she and my mother lost touch?'

'We make it a policy not to get involved in our residents' private lives,' Mrs Fay explained. 'Some of them have had rather colourful pasts that are, of course, none of our business. We are here to care for their day-to-day wellbeing, not to investigate their former lives.'

Issy suspected from the crisp reply that the company mission statement was something Mrs Fay had delivered several times.

'What time can I visit?' Issy asked.

'You're welcome whenever you wish. Our residents live in self-contained flats and come and go as they wish. Are you ringing from London?'

'Yes.'

'The train journey takes about an hour. Why don't you join Bella for coffee, say about eleven o'clock? She'll be ready by then. We have a private lounge so you'll be able to talk undisturbed.'

Hollies was a large, white-painted Regency structure near the Hove seafront. The taxi driver informed Issy that the complex had been developed from several residences.

'Some Victorian entrepreneur knocked three houses into one. He lived there for years, but when he passed on his family didn't want it, so the building and the surrounding land were sold to the highest bidder. Here we are.' He pulled up outside.

Issy's heart was thumping so loudly from nerves she was surprised he

125

couldn't hear it.

'Don't forget your flowers.' He picked up her bouquet of red roses. 'Are they for a relative?'

'My grandmother,' Issy said, still unused to the sensation of at last having a proper grandparent. Now she knew why Pat Dillaine's mother had expressed no interest in seeing her when she visited her son. She wasn't her grandmother. Bella Tucker was.

Issy stood at the foot of the steps and looked up at the building in front of her. A net curtain twitched at one of the windows.

'Ms Dillaine?' A pleasant, middle-aged woman greeted her. 'I'm Mrs Fay. Come in. Bella's all ready and waiting for you in the lounge. She was so excited when I told her about your visit. Would you like me to put your flowers in some water?' Chatting away, she led Issy down a long corridor. 'We had a conservatory built on several years ago,' she explained. 'It's extremely popular with the residents and their guests. It's bright and warm, and even on the coldest day it's sunny. Here we are.'

Issy stepped through and followed Mrs Fay to a comfortable corner of the conservatory. Seated in a wicker chair was a smartly-dressed lady who appeared to be asleep.

'Bella.' Mrs Fay raised her voice and touched her on the shoulder. 'Your visitor is here.' She turned back to Issy. 'I'll arrange coffee. Make yourself comfortable.'

Bella slowly opened her eyes. For a moment the two women looked at each other.

'Amy?' Bella raised her hand. 'It can't be.'

'I'm Amy's daughter, Issy.' She swallowed down the lump in her throat.

A cheerful assistant arrived with a tray of coffee and biscuits.

'You haven't taken off your coat.' The carer gave Issy a friendly smile. 'When the sun comes round it gets very warm in here.' She kept up a round of cheerful chatter as she laid the coffee table. 'You're in luck. Chef had a baking day yesterday. Look, Bella, your favourites.'

'Cherry cookies. How lovely.' Bella's eyes lit up.

'Don't hog them all. Remember your manners and share them with your granddaughter.'

'Have you met Issy? She's come all the way from London to visit.'

Bella put a hand over her mouth to disguise a yawn. The assistant cast Issy a sympathetic look.

'I don't think she slept very well. She kept pressing the office intercom to make sure we hadn't forgotten about your visit. I'll leave you to it.'

Issy draped her coat around the back of her chair and sat down.

Bella looked at her again. 'You're Amy's daughter?'

'That's right.'

'You've got the same colour hair.'

'Have I?'

'She was very like her mother. You all had blonde hair, so unusual.'

Issy frowned. Was this contact going to be yet another disappointment?

'I thought you were Amy's mother.'

'I was her stepmother, and although I tried, I never could take her mother's place. She died when Amy was five years old. Her father advertised for a housekeeper and I accepted the position. After a while, it seemed a sensible arrangement for Marco and I to get married. I don't think Amy ever really forgave her father for getting married again.' Bella chewed on a cherry cookie. 'She adored her father, and after I was widowed she proved too much of a handful for me to handle on my own. Always off out with her friends, going to parties and dances. Mind you,' Bella's face softened, 'she was a beautiful girl. When she was little and we were out shopping, people used to stop me in the street and comment on her lovely blonde hair.'

A shadow crossed Bella's face.

'I loved Amy, but to her I was only her stepmother.'

'I'm sorry,' Issy said softly. 'I'm sure in her own way she loved you.'

'Do you think so? We did have some good times together. The silly girl got herself into trouble, didn't she? She was so trusting.' Bella's voice trailed off as she became lost in her thoughts.

'Someone sent a monthly allowance to a bank account set up in my name. Was it you?' Issy asked in a careful voice.

'No, dear. It wasn't me.' Bella looked surprised at the suggestion. 'I didn't know where you were.'

Issy hesitated, reluctant to open old wounds.

'You knew Amy had a daughter?'

'She wrote me a note saying she was going away with you, but she didn't give me any details. I think she was ashamed to come home. I'm sorry we lost touch. We mustn't let it happen again. I'm so pleased I've found you.'

The morning clouds parted and the sun cast a ray across the colourful cork tiles that decorated the floor.

'Let's have coffee and cookies,' Bella suggested, 'and you can tell me all about yourself. We've a lot to catch up on.'

11

'This is all your fault.' Harry accosted Ed as he crossed the threshold of the hotel foyer.

'What is?' Ed struggled to release himself from Harry's hold as he grabbed the collar of his jacket.

'I'm in trouble with Roger.' Harry took no notice of Ed's protests as the two of them became entangled in an unseemly tussle.

'What are you talking about?' Ed tried to maintain his footing.

'As if you didn't know,' Harry sneered, 'Issy of course. Have you been filling her head with fancy ideas? Offering her a fortune for her story? Turning her head with tales of celebrity? You journalists are all the same.'

'I haven't seen her since you blew my cover.' Ed narrowly avoided colliding with a potted plant as he finally struggled free from Harry's clutches.

'Then where is she?'

'Excuse me, gentlemen,' the receptionist broke into their heated exchange. 'Would you please keep your voices down? You're upsetting the other residents.'

'Sorry,' Ed apologised, straightening his jacket collar. Harry glared and said nothing.

'I couldn't help overhearing,' the receptionist went on, 'are you talking about Ms Dillaine?'

'Issy, yes.' Ed leaned forward, eager to know more, but Harry elbowed him out of the way.

'Where's she gone?' Harry demanded.

'She received a letter from the hostel where she had been staying. The porter brought it over. Then this morning, Ms Dillaine asked my colleague to order a taxi for her to go to Victoria Station. There was a note in the logbook. Ms Dillaine said she didn't know when she would be back because she was going to visit her mother's mother.'

'What is going on?' Harry turned his

attention back to Ed.

'I have absolutely no idea.'

The receptionist cast an anxious look around the foyer. Ed dragged a protesting Harry into the bar and pushed him into a vacant seat. 'Now tell me exactly what you do know.'

'It was last night,' Harry muttered, 'late yesterday afternoon, actually. Remember our bust-up?'

'I'm not likely to forget it.'

'Issy got this message saying Don Dealy had been in touch?' Harry said, a querying note in his voice. 'You've heard of him, that celebrity who auditions wannabes on his talent show?'

'Go on,' Ed urged.

'She wanted to call him back, and said she would join me in the pizza parlour when she was through, only she didn't. I thought she'd gone off with you.'

'I haven't seen her since you told her Jonathan Jackson was my uncle. Thanks for that, by the way,' Ed muttered under his breath.

Harry dismissed his comment with a wave of his hand. 'Like I was saying, I was annoyed. Girls don't stand me up.'

'You don't say.' Ed crossed his arms, a sarcastic expression crossing his face. 'It must be your charm that wins them over every time.'

Harry threw back his head in a gesture of indignation. '*You're* not exactly full of the milk of human kindness . . . '

'I'm not about to start another fight; get on with it,' Ed urged when Harry looked as though he were about to attack him again. 'I haven't time for theatricals.'

With a glare at Ed, Harry continued, 'When it was obvious Issy wasn't going to join me in the pizza parlour, I sent her a text telling her that dinner was off.'

'And that's the last contact you had with her?'

'She texted back saying she was sorry, and that was that. I went out with some friends, then when I got back to the hotel I remembered Roger wanted to talk to us on the video link. I tapped on Issy's door but there was no reply. Roger wasn't best pleased, but there was nothing I could do apart from dragging Issy from her bed, which I didn't think was a good idea. Then this morning, I discover she's not in her room. According to reception she's gone to visit her grandmother. There you have it. You know as much as I do.'

Ed frowned. It wasn't easy keeping tabs on Issy. She didn't keep him in the frame, and now she knew Jonathan Jackson was his uncle their relationship was in tatters.

'What are you doing here anyway?' Harry broke into his thoughts.

'I came to see if I could make things up with Issy.'

'You'll be lucky. After what you did to her, your name's mud.'

'I doubt yours is squeaky clean.'

Harry rewound his scarf. 'Well, I'm not going to sit down all day and wait for her to reappear.'

Before Ed could detain him any longer, Harry leapt up out of his chair, strode through the double doors and out into the street.

With a sigh, Ed threw himself into Harry's seat. The day stretched in front of him. He'd made one or two enquiries about sponsorship on Lucinda's behalf, but he felt it was too soon to get in touch with her again. She could possibly be regretting having opened up so much at their last meeting. His mobile signified an incoming call.

'Ed?' Jonathan greeted him. 'How did you get on with Lucinda?'

'I'll tell you about it later,' Ed replied.

'Problems?'

'Not from Lucinda, no, but there have been developments. I've got news for you.'

'Go on.'

'I'm hearing tales that Issy is with her grandmother.'

'That means she must still be alive.'

'I'd already worked that one out for myself, Jonathan.'

'Funny, I was convinced Amy's mother died when she was a child.'

'Well, if the receptionist is to be believed, she didn't.'

'Wait, it's coming back to me now,' Jonathan said.

'What is?'

'Her family situation. Amy could speak fluent Italian because her father's mother came from Naples. That's how she landed her job at the airline. They're always looking for language skills. Where is this grandmother now?'

'According to reception, Issy ordered a taxi to take her to Victoria Station. She could have gone anywhere.'

'Probably somewhere on the south coast. No matter. Anything else bugging you?' Jonathan asked.

'The fact that Issy's found out about us didn't exactly make my day.'

'What's done is done. Obviously I would have preferred to keep her in the dark about our relationship for a little longer, but now she does know I suppose we all ought to get together.

Here's what I want you to do.' Jonathan paused. 'You are going to have to earn Issy's trust.'

'If I ever see her again.'

'Work on her.' Jonathan ignored the interruption.

'How?'

'A little flattery never went amiss.'

'Jonathan, you are so last century.' Ed's voice was full of scorn.

'I've never known a female not respond to a compliment.'

'You haven't met Issy, have you?' Ed asked in a stony voice.

'No.'

'Then let me inform you: telling her she looks beautiful in the moonlight will *not* work.'

'Don't be so defeatist,' Jonathan dismissed his nephew's protest. 'If you really can't come up with anything, then tell her the truth. I've always found honesty is the best policy.'

'The truth about what?'

'That you knew she would overreact if she learned you were my nephew, that you're very sorry you didn't tell her earlier, and that you didn't mean to deceive her; something along those lines. I'm sure you've had more experience than I have at this sort of thing.'

'I could try, I suppose,' Ed agreed reluctantly, scratching his chin. 'When I eventually catch up with her.'

'Why don't you invite her down to Burton Abbots? I'll square things with Cordelia. It's been a while since we've done any entertaining.'

'You're not serious?'

'Actually, you'd be doing us a favour. Cordelia's had a bit of a falling-out with our eldest, Penny. Her sister Sophie took Penny's side. It was no more than a silly spat but nobody wants to back down. If you and Issy were here, well, it might ease the tension between the girls. We'd have Ireland to talk about, and you could tell us about that award-winning piece you did on Afghanistan.'

'Things could turn nasty if you and

Issy don't hit it off.'

'Run it past her. I'm sure Issy would welcome the chance to see some of the English countryside. Is she interested in history?'

'Probably not. She's too modern for castles and dungeons and kings with old-fashioned names.'

'Then she'll click with Penny and Sophie. They can talk snow together.'

'I beg your pardon?'

'They're off skiing in a month's time. Issy will be able to give them tips.'

'I don't think she's ever been skiing.'

'She grew up in the wilds, didn't she? There's bound to have been some snow or a mountain somewhere about the place.'

'Geography never was your strong point, was it?' Ed replied, knowing it would do no good to try to dissuade his uncle from inviting Issy down to stay. Once he got an idea in his head, it was difficult to dislodge it.

'It's been ages since you've seen your cousins, too. Family is important and it doesn't do to let these things lapse. Fix a date and ring me back. Remember, Issy can only say no.'

Ed cut the connection with a thoughtful frown. On reflection, maybe it wasn't such a bad idea. He'd had plenty of experience facing challenges head-on. The only trouble was, he mused with a wry smile, none of them had involved Issy Dillaine.

'I'd like to leave a message for Ms Dillaine when she returns,' he told the girl on the desk.

'Certainly, sir.'

She passed over a pad. He chewed the pencil thoughtfully whilst he decided exactly what to say.

12

Issy awoke to the sound of seagulls mewling. She closed her eyes against the diamond-sharp brightness of the sky. A crisp breeze disturbed the net curtains fluttering in front of the open window. She snuggled down under the duvet and wriggled her toes. It was like the first day of term at school.

There was so much to look forward to, she didn't know where to start. When Mrs Fay offered her the use of the guest accommodation for a night's sleepover, Issy had leapt at the chance.

'If you're sure?'

'That's what it's there for,' Sally had insisted.

'I'll need to pop out for a few essentials,' Issy said.

'There are plenty of shops in Brighton. You'll find everything you need. Bella likes to rest in the afternoon, and as she didn't have a very good night's sleep it might be better not to tax her too much on your first day.'

After making her purchases Issy had spent the afternoon exploring the city. Wandering down The Lanes and looking in the windows of the exquisite specialist shops, she had become so engrossed in her surroundings she completely forgot the time. Refreshing herself with a cup of tea, she contacted the hotel to say she wouldn't be back until the next day.

'That's quite all right, Ms Dillaine,' the receptionist informed her. 'I'll make a note of it.'

'Are there any messages?'

'Mr Stanwood was here earlier. He would like you to contact him as soon as possible.'

'Right, well, I hope to be back some time tomorrow. If my plans change I'll be in touch.' Issy rang off.

Annoyed that she had so nearly fallen for Ed's urbane charm, her thoughts turned to Don Dealy as she wandered down to the seafront. The winter wind chafed her face and her throat ached from the raw, cold air, but she needed to have her senses stimulated by nature. There was much of her mother's life that was a mystery to her. Bella had shown her a new side to Amy and filled in a few gaps, but so much was still unexplained. Would she have embarked on this quest, she thought, if she'd known of the consequences? None the wiser, Issy turned away from the sea. Feeling cold, she called up a taxi for the journey back.

That evening, Bella didn't want to miss the latest episode of her favourite soap opera, after which some of the other residents had insisted on playing cards and board games. Bella had joined in, then was too tired for further conversation. Quelling her disappointment, Issy had kissed her goodnight before spending the rest of the evening reading up on Brighton's Regency past.

* * *

The next morning, a gentle tap on the door broke into her thoughts.

'Come in,' Issy called out.

A nursing assistant poked her head round the door.

'Good morning. I've brought you some tea.'

'Thank you, but you shouldn't have. You've got enough to do without waiting on me.'

'My pleasure.'

The fresh-faced girl entered the room and placed the tray on a chest of drawers.

'You're from Ireland?' she asked, an enquiring look on her face.

'Yes, I am.'

'I thought I recognised your accent.'

'Have you been to Ireland?'

'No, but I'd love to go'

'You'd like it.'

'I expect our cold weather makes you feel at home. Shall I pour?'

'Please.' Issy sat up and adjusted her new nightdress around her shoulders.

'No-one realised Bella had any

relatives. You're her granddaughter, aren't you?'

'She was my grandfather's second wife,' Issy explained.

'We're all pleased for her. She's a sweetie. There's never a cross word from her, and she always asks after us and our families, especially our boyfriends.' The girl gave a self-conscious giggle. 'What are your plans for the day?' She hovered by the door.

'I thought I'd take Bella out, perhaps for a walk along the seafront?'

'She'd like that. Enjoy your tea.'

The facilities in the guest accommodation were basic and it didn't take Issy long to wash and dress. It was still too early to pay Bella a visit so she opted for an early-morning stroll. Several joggers pounded the pavement as they ran past her, and an elderly gentleman accompanied by a toy poodle raised his hat and wished her good morning.

The headlines of a magazine on a newsagent's stand caught Issy's eye. On the front was a picture of a smiling Don

Dealy. The caption said he had been nominated for an entertainments industry award. A wry expression crossed Issy's face. The critics savaged Don's show, yet viewing figures were high. Professionally, it seemed Don was a person you loved to hate. Personally, she had to admit she liked him. He had shown her nothing but kindness despite Lucinda's odd behaviour. So many showbiz personalities had chequered private lives, but apart from the scandal involving Amy, Don was squeaky-clean.

Issy turned away from the seafront. It was time for coffee, and as she'd only had a cup of tea for breakfast, she was feeling hungry.

Bella was seated in her favourite corner of the conservatory, nibbling more cherry cookies.

'There you are, darling.' Her face lit up as Issy leaned forward to kiss her. 'Where have you been? I've been waiting hours for you.'

'I went for a walk,' Issy replied, taking one of the cookies.

'You shouldn't go out without telling me where you're going,' Bella chided.

'Sorry,' Issy apologised.

'I do worry about you.'

'There's no need,' Issy assured her with a bright smile.

'Of course there isn't. I'm being silly, I know. It used to drive Amy mad. Take no notice of me.'

'It's nice that you care.' Issy stroked her arm.

Bella beamed back at her.

'Mrs Fay said we're going out for a walk.'

'That's the plan if you feel up to it.'

'That's what I really miss, you know. Robbie was a great walker. We met on a ramble. He liked to stretch his legs. He was a sales rep for a cleaning products company and he used to have to do a lot of driving, so on his days off we'd put on our boots and tramp the Surrey countryside; Box Hill, Leith Hill, we did them all.'

Issy would have liked to ask more questions, but Sally had warned her not to tax Bella's memory.

'Don't rush things,' she'd said. 'Bella does tire easily.'

Bella leaned forward in her seat. 'There's a suitcase on top of my cupboard full of Amy's bits and pieces,' she confided. 'We'll go through it together some time. It hasn't been opened in years.'

'That would be lovely,' Issy agreed.

'Now, I'm ready if you are?' Bella wiped biscuit crumbs off her cardigan. 'Where's my coat?'

Well wrapped up against the winter chill, they ventured out onto the promenade, past the remains of the West Pier.

'It burnt down,' Bella explained. 'I wasn't living here then but I believe it was all very exciting. Now look at the poor old thing. It's nothing but a burnt-out skeleton.'

Issy sat beside Bella in one of the sheltered seats. The sea was calm and sparkled in the cold sunlight.

'I've heard you can see France on a

clear day,' Bella said. 'I'm not sure if it's true,' she added, catching the scepticism on Issy's face, 'but it makes a nice story.'

'Do you mind if I ask you questions?' Issy squeezed Bella's gloved hands. 'I'll stop if it's too much for you.'

'I'll answer them as best I can, but my memory does play tricks on me. Ask away and we'll see how we go.'

'Where did you live before you came here?'

'In a pretty cottage in a small village in Surrey. It was nice there, all leafy lanes and rolling hills. Of course there wasn't much for young people to do. I think that's why Amy got a job working for an airline. She looked so smart in her uniform. I was very proud of her. I've got a photo of her somewhere. Anyway, she got herself a little flat, it was more convenient for the airport you understand, and after that we didn't see an awful lot of her. Our worlds grew apart.'

Bella lapsed into silence. Gentle

waves lapped the shingle, as she closed her eyes. Issy got up and walked towards the railings. Several brave souls were trudging along the beach, well wrapped up against the elements. A father and son threw pebbles into the sea, the child squealing with excitement. The scene was reassuringly normal, an innocent break from the background turmoil of her personal life. She watched a speedboat sending up powerful spray as it cleaved through the water. Above them a helicopter hovered.

'Issy?'

Issy turned and hurried back to Bella, who complained: 'I'm getting cold.'

'Shall we go back and look through this suitcase of yours?' Issy suggested.

'People thought Amy was slow,' Bella said as they walked back their arms entwined. 'She wasn't. She was bright, an intelligent girl. Her therapist was a woman with progressive ideas; she recognised her condition before much was known about it. She taught Amy how to train her brain to recognise certain numbers.'

'What was that, Bella?' Issy faltered and nearly lost her footing, aware she had missed something important.

'Marco didn't like therapists. He was a bit old-fashioned when it came to that sort of thing, but I persisted.'

'Why was Amy having therapy?' Issy asked.

'These days they call it word blindness, except in her case it was numbers.'

'You mean Amy was dyslexic?' Issy raised her voice against the noise of the passing traffic.

'She used to transpose her figures,' Bella smiled, unaware of the turmoil her words had created, 'but the therapy sorted her out. They taught her special ways to remember numbers.'

As they approached the house, a people-carrier was parked outside and luggage was being loaded on board

'What's going on?' Bella asked.

'There you are.' Sally Fay greeted them with relief. 'I was afraid you wouldn't be back in time.'

'For what?' Issy asked.

'The transport,' Sally explained with her cheerful smile. 'I'd quite forgotten Bella's booked to go away for a few days to our holiday home further down the coast. The hairdresser is waiting to do her hair, then after a quick lunch we'll be off.'

13

'Where've you been?' Ed was pacing up and down the pavement outside Issy's hotel, his face pinched with cold. 'I've been hanging around for hours waiting for you.'

'Why?'

Despite her terse response to his greeting, Issy was pleased to see Ed's craggy, familiar face, even if his expression was dark and unwelcoming.

'Harry's full of some wild story about you having been kidnapped.' Without warning Ed drew Issy into his arms and hugged her. His stubble scratched her face. Issy tried to struggle free but she was powerless in his grip. Eventually she pushed him away. They were both breathing heavily as they faced each other, unsteady on their feet, each surprised by the intensity of their emotion.

'Kidnapped?' Issy responded after she'd got her breath back.

'By your grandmother,' Ed replied with a quirky smile. 'Tell me, was she toting a gun?'

'For goodness sake,' Issy pleaded, running a confused hand across her forehead, 'it's been a long day. Can we get inside?'

'It's all right. I didn't believe him.' Ed tagged along beside her. 'I didn't know you had a grandmother.'

'I haven't,' Issy replied.

'Another wild goose chase, was it? Don't worry, I'll make it up to you.'

'Welcome back, Ms Dilliane,' the receptionist greeted her.

Issy took her key and turned back to Ed.

'I haven't a clue what you're talking about but was there anything else?' she demanded in a cool voice, determined to douse her feeling of pleasure at seeing him again.

'My uncle wondered . . . ' Ed looked less sure of himself. ' . . . well, he's invited you down to Burton Abbots; that's his house in the country.'

Issy's mouth fell open.

'He's done what?'

'He would like to meet you. His wife's very sociable. She's called Cordelia and they've got two daughters, Penny and Sophie; they're my cousins. They're married, my cousins that is, so I hope you like babies. They've got three between them. You will come, won't you? You'll have a good time, honestly.'

'Where is this Burton Abbots?' Issy asked, wishing the prospect of a weekend in the country with Ed wasn't so appealing.

'Gloucestershire, it's a lovely part of the world. It's where they film all those English murder mysteries.'

'Hardly a glowing recommendation.'

'Come on, give it a go,' Ed coaxed, looked expectantly at Issy. 'You're a girl who likes a challenge.'

'I can't make a decision now. Don Dealy has invited me down to Swallow

House. He thought it would better if I visited when Lucinda was away.'

'Lucinda's not such a bad old bird,' Ed put in, 'especially when you fill her up with peppermint creams.'

'When were you filling her up with peppermint creams?' Issy's eyes narrowed in suspicion.

'I interviewed her,' Ed admitted. 'In the cause of research,' he added.

'Is there anything else you omitted to tell me, 'in the cause of research' or otherwise?'

'Dinner? Tonight?' Ed suggested. 'We could talk then.'

Issy opened her mouth to say she wasn't in the least bit hungry when her stomach emitted a loud growl. Ed smiled, sensing victory.

'Look, I'm sorry about all that's gone wrong between us. My uncle is really looking forward to meeting you. Won't you reconsider?'

'I'll think about it,' Issy replied, realising it would be churlish to turn down the invitation for the sake of it, and that maybe she should meet Jonathan Jackson.

'I'll ring him now.'

Issy pressed the button on the lift.

'Seven o'clock?' Ed said as the doors closed. 'See you in the foyer.'

As Issy was swept up to the second floor she inspected her reflection in the mirror. Surely meeting up with Ed hadn't stained her cheeks such a delicate shade of pink and brought a sparkle to her eyes?

★ ★ ★

Ed was waiting as Issy stepped out of the lift at a quarter past seven.

He looked smarter than usual in a blue shirt, denims and a leather jacket. Issy too had chosen her outfit with care. Too dressy would mean she was treating their dinner as a proper date, and that was not the idea. In the end she had gone for crimson trousers and a black top. She'd swept up her blonde hair into a bun, leaving a few loose tendrils to frame her face.

As she'd been getting ready, she had tried and failed to ignore her feminine side. It was telling her in no uncertain terms that she was looking forward to dinner with Ed.

'It's not far,' Ed greeted her, his eyes expressing his appreciation of her outfit, 'within walking distance.'

The night air was crisp, but the cold provided a welcome contrast to the overheated atmosphere of the hotel.

'I spoke to my uncle and he'll be pleased to see us any time,' Ed said.

'You're taking a lot for granted. I haven't officially accepted his invitation yet.'

'You will, though, won't you? Actually, Jonathan has an ulterior motive.'

'Thought he might have.' Issy cast an enquiring glance at Ed.

'Why do you say that?'

'Your uncle strikes me as the sort of person who doesn't do anything without good reason.'

'I think you're being a bit harsh on

him. He didn't have to answer your advert.'

'What's this ulterior motive?' Issy's voice softened.

'There's been a bit of unpleasantness between Cordelia and the girls.' Ed held up a hand. 'Don't ask what it's about, because I don't know. Too many feminine hormones, I expect.'

'That's the worst type of outdated sexist remark.' Issy flared up.

'Isn't it?' Ed grinned. 'But it's got you talking to me again.'

'I've a good mind to break our date.'

'So we're on a date, are we?'

'No, we're not.' Issy clenched her fists. She'd fallen neatly into his trap, and she didn't like the surge of pleasure it gave her when she argued with him.

'Anyway, Jonathan thinks our presence will defuse the atmosphere. I mean, they can hardly go at it hammer and tongs with us there, can they?'

'I suppose not,' Issy acknowledged.

Ed shivered.

'It's cold. Let's do shared body warmth.'

Before Issy could object, Ed slipped his hand through the crook of her elbow.

'That's better. Now, hurry up. I'm starving.'

'Won't your cousins wonder who I am and what I'm doing with you?' Issy demanded, doing her best to ignore the strength of Ed's muscles as he strode along beside her.

'Cordelia's always inviting people down for the weekend. I expect everyone will think you and I are an item.'

'Well, they can just un-think that idea right now or the visit's off,' Issy insisted.

'Whatever you say,' Ed agreed hurriedly.

He pushed open the door to the restaurant. The smell of a rich onion-and-tomato sauce wafted towards them.

'I booked a table,' Ed explained to the waiter who came forward to greet them.

'Mr Stanwood?' He consulted his

bookings, then picked up two menus. 'May I say how much I enjoy your work?'

Issy cast a surprised look at Ed. She had meant to look him up on the Internet, but so much had happened since she arrived it had slipped her mind.

'Thank you,' Ed replied with a modest smile.

The waiter led them across the room to a small table in an alcove lit by an ornate lamp. Issy couldn't help noticing several glances cast in their direction, mainly from female diners. She was glad now she had chosen to wear her crimson trousers and black top. The outfit perfectly fitted the occasion.

'Hope you like pasta,' Ed said as they sat down. 'I have to admit the smell of that sauce is tingling my tastebuds.'

'Tingling your tastebuds?' Issy raised an eyebrow. 'I had no idea you were so poetic; or,' she added, 'so well known.'

One or two diners raised their glasses to him.

'I'm not,' Ed insisted, and hid his face behind the menu. 'I'm an under-cover guy.'

After they had ordered, Issy leaned back in her seat.

'What do we do now?' she asked.

'What say we forget about our personal issues and get to know each other a bit better?' Ed suggested.

'All right,' Issy acknowledged, 'you go first.'

Ed swallowed some wine.

'I'm a Sagittarian, born in Yorkshire. My father was a railway clerk and my mother a dinner-lady. I have one brother, and we choose to meet up once in a blue moon.'

'Are your parents alive?'

'My mother is. She still lives up north. I've tried to persuade her to move nearer to my brother and me, but she won't hear of it. Her roots are in Yorkshire and she's happy there.'

'Your mother,' Issy began. 'She's Jonathan's brother?'

'I know what you're going to say

next. How come he was a QC and she a lowly dinner-lady?'

'I wasn't going to put it like that,' Issy protested.

'But you'd like to know? Jonathan was ambitious. He worked hard at school and won a scholarship. Then, when he married Cordelia, he leapt up the social scale. Her family can trace their ancestors way back goodness knows how far. That doesn't mean to say Jonathan has forgotten his roots.'

'Doesn't Cordelia's background make things difficult for your side of the family when you do meet up?'

'Mum won't venture further south than Leeds; so no, not really.'

'What about your brother?'

'He's a rugby player and travels a lot. I don't think Jonathan has been in touch with him in ages. So there you have it.'

'Don't you have any warts?' Issy enquired.

Ed raised an eyebrow. 'I don't think

now is the right time to discuss that sort of thing.'

'I meant in your past.'

'OK,' he said, pondering for a few moments. 'One of the masters at school didn't like me and gave me a bad English report,' he admitted.

'That must have dented your confidence.'

'It did — until I filled his favourite pen with vanishing ink. It was the one he used to write his damaging reports.'

'You did what?' Issy spluttered.

'It was the right thing to do.' Ed's face was full of moral outrage at the memory.

'Why were you so mad at him?'

'He marked me down out of spite, but my essay was a good piece of work — challenging and thought-provoking — and I wasn't having any of that.'

'Weren't your parents annoyed?'

'My mother was, but my father understood. He was all for the rights of the individual and he knew I wouldn't have done what I did without good reason; but, hey, I'm grateful to that teacher.'

'You are?'

'He made me realise the power of the written word, and like my dad, I stick up for the man in the street.'

'I'm impressed,' Issy acknowledged, 'by your principles.'

'Your turn now,' Ed urged. 'Tell me about your warts.'

'I was a victim of the school bully,' Issy admitted.

'That's tough,' Ed sympathised. 'Bet you took her on and won.'

'We were going on this field trip. All the other kids had new anoraks and dinky trainers with flashing lights?'

'Got it.' Ed nodded.

'I wore my dad's old checked jacket and a pair of moon boots that had holes in them. There was this girl who was always sneering at me. She was the ringleader.'

The waiter created an interruption by sprinkling fresh cheese onto their pasta. In the discreet lighting of the restaurant

Ed's deep brown eyes were doing a good job of making Issy forget she should hate him.

'I know this may be a question I'm going to regret asking, but what did you do?'

Issy spiked a pasta shell with her fork and chewed hard on it.

'Do you know how cold the Atlantic can be even in the height of summer?'

'I've a good idea.'

'When Sheila decided to take her unscheduled dip, everyone was most surprised. Her new trainers were ruined. The cream on the cake was, she got detention because the teacher thought she was showing off and had done it on purpose.'

'I suppose you didn't own up?'

'I didn't do anything,' Issy protested. 'She tripped and fell in.'

'Of course she did.'

'Well, I might have been a little bit instrumental in making sure she tripped over, but I never pushed her into the water.'

'Your secret is safe with me,' Ed assured her. He put a hand out and stroked her arm. 'Now, can I tempt you to dessert? The ice cream here is to die for.'

A violin began playing in the corner of the room. It was a tune Issy knew well, reminding her of summer evenings at home when everyone at the dig wound down for the day and began to relax.

'You don't dance, do you?'

To her surprise, Ed stood up and held out his hand. The next moment she was being led to the small postage-stamp-sized dance floor. He held her in his arms and twirled her round gently in time to the music.

'How am I doing?' he murmured in her ear.

'Where did you learn to dance?' Issy murmured back.

'A good journalist never reveals his sources.'

'Is that the only reply I'm going to get?'

'Maybe I'll tell you more at Burton Abbots.'

'In that case,' Issy replied with a reluctant smile, 'tell your uncle I accept his invitation.'

14

Don Dealy was waiting for Issy when she emerged from the dank booking hall out into the early afternoon sunlight. The sun caught the paintwork of his bright red Italian sports car parked in the area reserved for railway employees. He tooted his horn loudly and called her name. Several heads turned his way.

It was obvious Don enjoyed being the centre of attention, and the over-the-top greeting was as much for his benefit as Issy's.

He was dressed in a white shirt, the top three buttons left undone, and expensive designer jeans. For all his casual appearance it was obvious his dark hair had been freshly-styled, and his topped-up tan bore evidence of a recent session under the sunlamp.

With a charming smile, he chatted to

two giggling young mothers pushing baby buggies and signed his name on their shopping lists for them.

'We really enjoy your show,' one of them gushed.

'We vote every week,' the other put in.

'Keep them coming,' he smiled again. 'No votes, no show. Now if you'll excuse me, ladies, I have to attend to my guest.'

Two pairs of enquiring eyes turned in Issy's direction.

'Darling, how are you? Mwah.' He air-kissed Issy's cheeks; then, with a wicked twinkle in his eye, murmured in her ear: 'People expect me to go over the top, so I don't disappoint.' He squeezed her elbow. 'But I can do much better than an air-kiss. How about a proper embrace — that's if you don't mind?'

Before she could respond, Issy was crushed in a bear hug that had her struggling for breath.

Eventually Don released her.

'There are dark circles under your eyes.' He frowned, still holding her elbow. 'Has someone been giving you a tough time?'

'I'm fine,' Issy insisted.

'Remember, I'm here for you,' Don insisted, flicking a finger under her chin.

Issy decided to go for a bit of flattery. 'Congratulations on your award.'

'I haven't got it yet.' Don did his best to look modest, but as a diversionary tactic it worked. 'Now, we are going to have the most fantastic time.' He opened the passenger door. 'I thought you'd like the roof down. Have you got something for your hair? Meet the boys.' He gestured to the two dogs on the back seat. 'Buster and Barney.' Their tails thumped the leather upholstery in acknowledgement of the introduction.

While Don started the engine, Issy crammed a beanie on her head. He eased the car forward, acknowledging a group of bystanders at the traffic lights. 'I don't talk much while I'm driving,' he confided as he put his foot down on the accelerator. Issy's seatbelt tightened and held her fast as they took off. 'Enjoy the ride.'

The countryside sped past. All Issy could remember from her last visit to Swallow House was a series of strange shapes looming at her in the dark from the back of a dingy taxi.

Today, spring was pulling out the stops. She'd read that Kent was known as 'The Garden of England', and in broad daylight she could understand why. Oast houses nestled beside ivy-clad cottages, and although the air smelt of frost, clumps of green shoots were pushing through the grassy wayside verges.

Issy raised her face to the winter sun, glad to be out of London.

'Here we are. Would you mind opening up, Issy?' Don slowed down outside a pair of wrought-iron gates and gave her a key.

Swallow House looked less threatening in the early-afternoon sunshine than it had in the depths of a winter's night. Issy stepped out of the car and unlocked the gates. She stood back as Don drove through, then refastened the padlock to the chain linked through the railings.

'Hate to have to do that,' Don explained as she got back in the car, 'but if we don't secure them, fans stroll down the drive at all hours of the day and night. We've had cameras thrust through the open windows while we've been having dinner. Once, a photographer fell out of a tree and landed at my feet when I was walking the dogs. So unless we're expecting guests, it's the way it has to be. Anyway, enough about that.' Don spattered gravel under his tyres as he screeched to a halt in front of the oak door decorated with its distinctive bullfrog knocker. 'Jump out, then we'll have tea. I would offer something a little stronger, but I'm filming again next week, and puffy eyes in front of the camera I do not need.'

Don put a hand under Issy's elbow

and guided her into the hall.

'I don't expect you remember much from your last visit, but this time it's going to be different. I'm all yours. I've told Mrs Hammond not to put through any calls and to turn away all visitors.'

The conservatory faced the back of the house and no expense had been spared with the furnishings. Luxurious wicker chairs boasted an assortment of colourful rugs and vivid scatter cushions. Paintings adorned the walls and Turkish carpets covered the flagstones. The window ledges were crammed with a riot of elaborate pot plants.

'I hope you like my telescope.' Don swung the lens skywards, reminding Issy of a small boy showing off his new toy. 'I like to look at the heavens after a day of dealing with artistic temperaments. It helps remind me I'm no bigger than the smallest insect in the mechanics of things.' Don laughed at the expression on Issy's face. 'I'm not as nasty as I'm made out to be. It's a big act.'

The coffee table was laden with awards and polished shields.

'Now, make yourself comfortable.'

The housekeeper entered carrying a loaded tea tray.

'We'll help ourselves, thank you, Mrs Hammond,' Don said.

'Don't forget your tablets, sir,' she murmured in his ear as she placed the tray on a low table.

'A lot of fuss about nothing,' Don insisted, catching Issy's look of concern. 'One of those silly stress-related scares, nothing more.' He brushed aside her anxiety with a wave of his hand. 'I take no notice of it, and hope it will recognise it is not wanted and shove off. Would you mind pouring the tea? I'll have China with a slice of lemon, please; it makes it easier to swallow these disgusting pink pills the doctor's given me. I'm sure they don't do any good, but as the studio's paying for his medical services, even I have to do as I'm told on occasions.'

Issy attended to the tea while Don

swallowed his capsules.

'Not on a diet, are you?'

Issy shook her head.

'Then help yourself.'

Issy spread some raspberry jam onto a scone. She wasn't hungry but she needed to keep her hands occupied. She had questions to ask and she wasn't sure how Don would feel about answering them.

'Is it too soon to start asking about my mother?' she began.

'Talking about Amy and what happened is not something I do very often,' Don admitted. 'I've rather got out of the habit; but that's why you're here, isn't it? Ask away.'

'I don't know much about you either, or your wife.' Issy decided on a gentle approach.

'That's an easy one to start with. When we first met, Lucinda was the big star. Her career was going places. I was an extra in a crowd scene, totally out of her orbit, but we got chatting one day during a lull in shooting. There's always a lot of hanging around during filming. Anyway, she'd come out of her caravan to stretch her legs. I was lounging about doing nothing in particular, and we clicked from the off. She was stunningly beautiful, funny and clever. By the end of the shoot I'd fallen hopelessly in love. Of course, I knew I didn't stand a chance with her. Ours is a hierarchical business. She was the leading lady, I was a jobbing actor; so after the director had a word with me I backed off, but Lucinda was having none of that. She sought me out over coffee the next day, and soon we were an item.

'The press weren't very kind to me, as you can imagine. They called me all sorts of names. Anyway, one weekend during a break in filming, we sneaked off on the quiet and got married.'

'That must have rocked the boat.'

'The studio weren't best pleased, but the resultant publicity did them no harm; and in time, when people realised I intended to do right by my wife, I was accepted. Lucinda and I rode the storm and we've been very happy together.' Don regarded Issy with a thoughtful look on his face. 'Shall I go on with my story?'

'Please.'

'It's not common knowledge,' Don confided, 'but Lucinda's five years older than me. Gradually, starring roles began to dwindle. Youth is the name of the game in the entertainment industry. There's always a fresher face ready to step into your shoes. Lucinda was passed over for several roles she thought were in the bag. Not being one to sit around doing nothing, when her agent stopped ringing she set up her arts festival and theatre workshop. Lucinda absolutely loves what she does, so it turned out for the best. By the way,' Don flashed Issy a smile, 'if I'm going too fast for you, feel free to interrupt.'

'When did you get your big break?'

'It was one of those funny turns life sometimes takes. My agent said they wanted someone to front a talent show.

It didn't sound my sort of thing, but Lucinda insisted I try for it as several outstanding bills needed to be paid, so I went along. They whittled the list down to two, me and this other actor. He was far more experienced than me, full of charm and confidence, and I could see he thought the part was his. I realised I'd have to do something different to get noticed, so I sneered at him and pulled holes in his performance. He turned on me; really ugly, it was. I kept my cool but, suspecting I'd blown it, smiled at the producers and told them they knew where to contact me. Then I left.

'The next day my agent rang. I was expecting to be fired, but to my surprise he told me the producers liked what they saw. They asked if I could incorporate my sneers into the act. That was six years ago.'

'And you haven't looked back since?'

'The role reversal's been tough for Lucinda, but she's been very supportive and we'll always be a team.'

Issy nibbled her scone then licked jam off her fingers before asking, 'You and Lucinda don't have children?'

'A great disappointment to us both.'

Although Don had invited questions, Issy sensed she had touched on a delicate subject.

'I wondered why the nursery was so well-decorated?'

'We explored various options, and once or twice we came close to adoption, but in the end nothing came of it.' Don shrugged. 'Lucinda would have made a wonderful mother.'

Don's body language told Issy it was the only explanation she was going to get.

'To compensate, we've always surrounded ourselves with vibrant, talented people. Did you know your mother was an accomplished amateur artist?'

'I found some sketches amongst her things.'

'She possessed a natural talent for detail. She would do caricatures of our guests, and at times she could be a little bit naughty. If someone had bushy eyebrows she'd draw them very accurately but in such a way as not to cause offence. She was a lovely girl,' Don said, with a faraway look in his eyes.

'And Roger Street? How did you meet him?'

A shadow passed over Don's face.

'Lucinda's always involved in various projects, and he sort of appeared one day. I assumed he was one of her contacts, and by the time I realised my mistake, it was too late.' Don leaned forward. 'I'll tell you something I've never told another living soul, Issy. I wish I'd had the courage of my convictions and thrown him out when I realised I didn't like him or his so-called friends. It would have saved much heartache.'

'He's been trying to get in touch with me on a video link.'

For a moment Don said nothing.

'Then, darling,' when he finally spoke he looked unnaturally serious, 'I must caution you to be very careful indeed. Don't have any more to do with him than you absolutely have to.'

'I only want to find out about my mother. Is that so very wrong?' Issy pleaded.

'Not at all.' Don put his hand over hers. 'But it's important to know whom you can trust.'

Before Issy could speak, there was the sound of frantic barking.

'You did lock the front gates, didn't you?' Don asked.

'You saw me,' she replied.

'Then I'd better see what's upsetting the dogs.'

The next moment the conservatory door was swept open. Buster and Barney raced through, toppling a Greek statuette off its pedestal. Issy watched in frozen horror as it fell to the ground with a crash. Don, too, seemed frozen to the floor. Out of the corner of her eye, Issy caught a movement in the doorway.

It was Lucinda.

15

'Darling.' Don leapt into life. 'We weren't expecting you. You remember Issy, don't you?' he prompted his wife with an anxious smile.

The same wary expression Issy had noticed on her last visit clouded Lucinda's blue eyes.

Buster and Barney continued to chase each other around the conservatory, now dragging a trailing plant off the window ledge.

'Out,' Don bellowed.

'I'll see to the mess, sir.' Mrs Hammond ushered Buster and Barney out of the conservatory.

'And may we have some fresh tea?'

'Certainly, sir.'

'So.' Don cleared his throat after Mrs Hammond had picked up the tray and departed. 'You decided to come back early, darling?'

'My meeting was cancelled.'

'What a shame.'

'The fundraiser got cold feet, said he'd overextended himself and couldn't provide the backing he had promised.'

'I hope you're not too disappointed.'

'It happens.'

All the time she was speaking, Lucinda's eyes never left Issy's face. She raised a hand and took a step towards Issy.

'Darling,' Don cautioned his wife. With a fleeting glance at her husband, Lucinda let her hand drop to her side.

The ticking of the French clock on the dresser was the only sound to break the ensuing silence. It heightened the tension in the room. Aware she was clenching her hands, Issy relaxed her knuckles, smiled hesitantly at Lucinda, and waited for her to speak.

'I hope you haven't been indiscreet, Don.'

'Sorry?'

'Ed Stanwood is a friend of Issy's. You know, that journalist?'

Issy cast an anxious glance in Don's direction.

'Have you been talking to the press, Issy?' he asked with a frown.

'Ed isn't really the press. He contacted me after he read my advert,' Issy hurried to explain.

'Do you know about his uncle?' Lucinda asked in a careful voice.

'I know he's Jonathan Jackson.' Issy was pleased to see Lucinda looked less confident of herself.

'Why don't we all take the weight off our feet?' Don did his best to make light of the situation. 'I'm sure there are questions you'd like to ask Issy,' he smiled at his wife, 'and I know Issy has lots of things she'd like to ask us.'

'The only question I would like to ask Issy,' Lucinda disregarded her husband's invitation to sit down, 'is: why is she here?'

'Issy is here at my invitation,' Don explained.

'Have you explained about Finlay?' Lucinda asked.

Issy frowned.

'Who's Finlay?' she asked.

'He was my brother. It was because of your mother he went out on the lake that day. It was because of her he had his accident. Your mother broke his heart and he couldn't live without her.'

16

The drive from London to Burton Abbots took over two hours.

'I'm hardly ever in one place long enough to have a car of my own,' Ed explained as he picked Issy up outside her hotel. 'So I hired one.' He patted the sturdy steering wheel of the four-door saloon. 'It's not quite as racy as Don's Italian number, but there wasn't much choice. It seems everyone wants to get out of London for the weekend.'

Issy did her best to relax in the passenger seat. She had considered cancelling the trip, but a charming text from Jonathan Jackson telling her how much he and Cordelia were looking forward to meeting up with her had persuaded her to change her mind.

It was the first time she had seen Ed since the night they had danced together, and her feelings towards him were as jumbled as ever.

'By the way, I'm sorry about Harry Willetts,' Ed apologised as he started up the engine, 'but he got up my nose.'

'He was one of the main leads to my mother and you hacked him off brilliantly. Well done.'

Issy was pleased she had a reason to keep their relationship on a less personal basis.

'I said I'm sorry,' Ed repeated.

'You shouldn't have let him get to you. You're supposed to be the professional investigator.'

'My professional instincts told me he was spinning you a line. Most conmen are easy to believe, that's why they're so good at it. He and Roger Street proved to be no exception to the rule.'

'Thanks to you, Harry's done a runner.'

'What do you mean?'

'I haven't heard from him in days, and he was my only connection to Roger Street.'

'That doesn't surprise me. Things were getting too hot to handle for both of them, I should imagine.'

'The desk told me Harry had gone away for a few days. No-one was sure where or when he was coming back.'

'Last time I saw him he was panicking like mad, saying he wanted out. Remember, that time you went down to visit your grandmother?'

'Step-grandmother,' Issy corrected him, then wished she hadn't. Bella had shown her nothing but kindness.

'We are still friends, aren't we?' Ed pleaded.

Issy cast him a sideways glance. She had never been very good at holding grudges, and of the two men she had to admit she trusted Ed more than Harry. Relenting, she crooked her little finger in a gesture of friendship. Ed did the same and tweaked hers.

'Glad we've got that over with,' he sighed in relief. 'So, what's new?'

'Jonathan sent me a text; did you know?'

'I gave him your mobile number after I updated him about Harry and me.' Ed gave an embarrassed smile. 'He tore me off a strip and said I'd behaved like a fool, and some other stuff that you don't want to hear. He was totally out of order.'

'I'm beginning to like the sound of your uncle.'

'He's another one with buckets of charm,' Ed said in a wry voice.

'Pity it doesn't run in the family,' Issy responded as Ed eased up on the accelerator.

'Want to take a comfort break?' He indicated the service station exit coming up. 'Stretch your legs?'

'I ought to get Cordelia a thank-you gift,' Issy said. 'In all the fuss, I forgot.'

'You don't have to,' Ed insisted.

'Did you bring her anything?'

''Fraid I forgot, too.'

'Typical male. Then it'll have to be filling-station flowers. Come on.'

Armed with a pile of fashion magazines, flowers and a box of chocolates Ed had purchased at the Belgian confectionary outlet, they clambered back into the car. Peeling the foil off a bar of chocolate, Issy broke off a chunk.

'Tell me more about your uncle and aunt,' she said, chewing on it as Ed eased their car back onto the motorway.

'Cordelia and Jonathan have lived at Burton Abbots for years, ever since Penny and Sophie were small. It used to be a farmhouse, and there are outbuildings and an annex. It's situated in a lovely village with fantastic views over the surrounding countryside.'

'You sound like a real estate agent on a commission,' Issy teased Ed. 'You'll be telling me about the pony in the paddock next.'

Ed grinned back. 'Where was I?'

'Is the house haunted?'

'Not to my knowledge. Why do you ask?'

'I got the feeling Swallow House is haunted.'

'You mean you saw a ghost?'

'I felt a presence.'

'No kidding?'

'It was in the nursery when I was on the rocking horse. I felt unbelievably happy, like a child on her birthday.'

'Do you often get these feelings?'

'It's the first time it's ever happened to me.'

'I always thought ghosts wore black robes and moaned a lot and shook chains at people.'

'This one didn't. It pushed me gently backwards and forwards on my rocking horse.'

'Now you *have* lost the plot,' Ed scoffed.

Issy nibbled on some more chocolate. 'I wouldn't have expected you to understand. You weren't there. But there was definitely something about that room.'

'Do you think the nursery was ever used?'

'It had lots of books that looked unread and toys that didn't look as though anyone had played with them.'

'Something else that doesn't make sense. The list is growing daily.'

'And we are going round in circles. Tell me more about Burton Abbots,' Issy said, changing the subject.

'It's a family house really, and too big for Jonathan and Cordelia now that the girls have left home, but Cordelia doesn't want to move. All her friends live locally and it's convenient for Jonathan's golf course. There's also a large garden with a summerhouse. I caught Penny there once.' Ed grinned at the memory. 'It was her eighteenth birthday party and she was mad about this boy.'

'Were you spying on her?'

'Not at all, but she wasn't with the boy she was mad about. It seems it was a frantic attempt to make him jealous. I barged in on them, and I'm afraid I rather ruined things.'

'Now, there's a first.'

'I wasn't supposed to be there, but to be honest I'd had enough of her party. They weren't really my friends and I was looking for somewhere to crash out for a while. Things got a bit crowded in the summerhouse when the boy she was mad about turned up and demanded to know what was going on. I had to calm everyone down. After both boys stormed off, Pen and I shared a bottle of champagne she'd managed to snaffle from the bar. We still laugh about it to this day.'

'Which one did she marry?' Issy asked.

'Neither. She went backpacking to South America; but that's a story that's going to have to wait for another day,' Ed slowed down and turned off the motorway, 'because there's not far to go now. No need to be nervous,' he said, catching Issy's look of apprehension.

'Why do you think your uncle really wants to see me this weekend?'

'He didn't say.'

'You don't think . . . ' Issy began, then shook her head.

'What?' Ed prompted.

'That he believes my mother was

guilty and he wants to break the news to me gently?'

'It's more likely he wants to tell you his version of events. He knows about Don and Roger having been in touch. He may give you a new angle.'

'So far, no-one's given me the same story.'

'That's not surprising. It was a long time ago. People's memories play tricks.'

'I've been told my mother was beautiful, innocent, charming, manipulative and dyslexic. She confused her numbers. That must mean she was innocent, mustn't it?' Issy appealed to Ed.

'Not necessarily. I hate to disillusion you, but she would have been used to learning things by heart.'

'How do you know that?'

'Word association? She must have gone through a selection process for her job. If she managed to convince the interview board that she didn't have number blindness, then she was quite a clever cookie, wouldn't you say?'

Ed swung the car to the left, bumped down a rocky country lane and rolled to a halt outside a five-barred gate. He wound down the window and pressed a security button concealed in a wooden post.

'We're here,' he bellowed into a crackly speaker at the side of the double-fronted gates.

They creaked open and Ed moved forward down the drive. A petite woman with a pageboy haircut stood beside a grey-haired man on the doorstep of the house, her arms raised in welcome.

'Darlings,' Cordelia greeted them with a warm smile. 'We were beginning to wonder where you were.'

'We're not late, are we?' Ed raised a hand in greeting.

'Not at all. It's me, darling. I hate motorways. I always worry when guests are expected.'

Ed kissed his aunt and shook hands with his uncle.

'This must be Issy.' Cordelia held out her arms and kissed Issy on both cheeks. 'What lovely hair. I always wanted to be a blonde,' she raised her eyebrows theatrically, 'but I got dealt the mousey hair package.'

'My wife has coloured her hair so often we've all forgotten what it originally looked like,' Jonathan butted in with a friendly smile. 'Jonathan Jackson,' he introduced himself.

His handshake was firm and his smile eased Issy's anxieties.

'These are for you, Mrs Jackson.' Issy passed over their presents.

'For goodness sake, my name's Cordelia,' she protested. 'No need to be so formal. I always think of my mother-in-law when people call me Mrs Jackson; not that I don't love her to bits,' she added, with a sly glance at her husband, 'sometimes.'

'That's my grandmother you're talking about,' Ed protested.

'Let's all get inside. The girls aren't due until later, so we can have a leisurely lunch without interruptions.'

Jonathan took charge and ushered everyone through to the dining room.

'Thank you for the magazines.' Cordelia linked arms with Issy. 'I shall enjoy reading them. I do try to keep up with modern trends, but my daughters keep telling me I'm hopelessly out-of-date with fashions and celebrities.'

'When you're all on speaking terms,' Jonathan remarked over his shoulder. 'They've had words,' he murmured in an aside to Issy. 'Don't get involved.'

The intercom buzzed.

'Who on earth can that be?' Cordelia tutted.

'Mum,' a female voice wailed, 'open the gates. We're here.'

'Penny?' Cordelia shrieked in response.

'Sophie's with me. The men have gone off on a male bonding trip and we've parked the children on our in-laws. So we're all yours.'

'You're early,' Cordelia squawked. 'What am I going to do?' she hissed at her husband.

'Tell you what,' Jonathan offered, 'why don't Issy and I make ourselves scarce? Ed, stay with your aunt and act as referee between her and the girls if you need to.'

'Why me?' Ed protested.

'Because if I intervene, you can bet your bottom dollar it will wind up being my fault.'

'If I must,' Ed relented. 'Come on, Aunty, into the lions' den.'

'Honestly, my daughters really are the limit,' Cordelia protested. 'I told them teatime. I've nothing prepared for their lunch.'

'I'm sure you'll manage,' Ed soothed her. 'Let's walk down the drive and open the gates manually before they start climbing over them. See you later, guys.'

'I'll get us something to drink, Issy.' Jonathan bustled over to the table and snatched up a bottle of wine and two glasses. 'Better get some nibbles as well. When Cordelia and the girls get going, they are liable to forget all about us. We could starve to death in the summer-house.'

Issy stepped out onto the terrace. Water bubbled out of a sprite's mouth into an ornamental birdbath. She could see great care had been taken with the layout of the flagstones. The sun warmed her arms and she gave a contented sigh.

'Ready? It's this way.'

Jonathan led Issy through the flower-beds, past another water feature and down some steps.

'Here we are.' They came to a stop outside a round wooden building. 'We have to keep it locked now after we discovered a tramp was using it as a sleepover place last winter. He'd been here a week before anyone noticed. In the old days it wouldn't have happened. The girls were always conducting illicit liaisons in the summerhouse, but when they went off to get married, the poor old place rather got neglected, so Cordelia and I decided it was due a makeover. What do you think?'

He swung the door open. Issy stepped inside.

'It's lovely.'

Bright scatter rugs adorned the floor, and Issy could see from the dents in the cushions on the wicker seats that someone was a frequent visitor.

'I come here if Cordelia and I need a bit of space. I've got a radio, and I listen to the cricket or a bit of classical music and do the crossword. Sit down. Make yourself comfortable.'

Jonathan bustled around sorting out their drinks and the snacks he'd purloined from the dining room.

'Here we are.'

He settled down opposite Issy. She wriggled, uncomfortable with his scrutiny of her face.

'I'm sorry,' Jonathan apologised. 'I didn't mean to stare but you are so like your mother. It's like walking back in time.'

'What did you think of her?' Issy asked in a tremulous voice.

'I only saw her once but I was struck

by her beauty,' Jonathan replied. 'In those days I was very much the backroom boy.'

'Do you think she was innocent?'

'Honest answer? I really can't be sure. She liked the good life. She may have been in debt. Who knows?'

'Do you think Roger Street was a serious player in the scam?'

'Without a doubt. My enquiries revealed some very dubious contacts. Last I heard he was in Australia, but my nephew tells me he's been in touch?'

'Yes. He paid an out-of-work actor to pretend to be his half-brother.'

'That sounds exactly the sort of thing I would expect him to do. I also expect he was seriously spooked when he discovered you were on his case.'

'I wasn't,' Issy insisted. 'All I wanted to do was find out about my mother.'

'May I ask what started you off?'

'I didn't know I had been adopted until my parents died.'

'Ed tells me you were living in Ireland?'

'Amy moved there, I suppose to get away from all the attention, but I don't remember her. Relatives adopted me, and when I was going through their things I found a newspaper cutting and a few personal papers.'

'That must have been very distressing for you.'

'It had to happen sometime,' Issy replied.

'You know I was the one who got Ed involved, don't you?' Jonathan smiled. 'You could say I'm the cause of all the trouble, so I'll understand if you don't want my help, but if there's anything I can do . . . ?'

'Your nephew tells me you've taken up amateur sleuthing?'

'Not seriously,' Jonathan replied. 'I've traced a neighbour's lost cat and found a stolen bicycle in the river, that sort of thing, but I was rather taken by your advert.'

'You were working on the prosecution case?'

'That's right, but it never came to

trial, although Amy was cautioned. I was helping out with the paperwork, finding out all I could about the background of the case. It was horrendously complicated and most of our leads were dead ends. It's no wonder the whole thing collapsed. Unofficially, I was very glad it did. Whatever was going on, Amy wasn't the ringleader.'

A gentle tapping on the window interrupted them.

'Sorry to disturb you.' Ed poked his head through the open door.

'Is it safe to come out of hiding?' Jonathan enquired.

Ed cast an anxious look at Issy.

'Has something happened?' his uncle demanded.

'There's been a newsflash. Sorry, Issy.'

A sharp pain stabbed Issy's ribcage. Jonathan put out a hand to steady her.

'I don't know how to tell you,' Ed continued. 'Cordelia sent me down here to break it to you.'

'For goodness sake, boy,' Jonathan

snapped, 'put the pair of us out of our misery and tell us what's going on.'

'Don Dealy's suffered a heart attack.'

'Is he in hospital?' Issy gasped.

'He was.' Ed's voice was so gentle Issy could hardly hear what he was saying. 'He passed away just after ten this morning.'

17

'I wouldn't hear of you going back to your lonely hotel room,' Cordelia insisted when Ed broke the news to his aunt of Issy's intention to return to London. 'What can you do there that you can't do here?'

'I have to find out what happened to Don,' Issy said.

'Then use my laptop,' Cordelia replied, 'there are masses of tributes online.'

'I don't want to disrupt your plans for the weekend.'

'You won't. We'll have a quiet supper tonight, and if you can't face the family tomorrow then you can have something on a tray in your room, but we will not leave you on your own for one moment. You poor darling, what a horrible time you are having.'

Unused to such kindness, it was all

Issy could do not to break down. She couldn't believe she would never see Don again. Although she hardly knew him he had been a significant presence in her life.

'The girls have gone visiting an old school friend and won't be back until later, so I suggest that instead of staring at a computer screen all afternoon, you and Ed go for a nice long walk. Then, when you come back, we'll do comfort food — buttered jacket potatoes and baked beans? How does that sound?'

'Cordelia, you are ace.' Ed kissed his aunt's cheek.

'Then off you go. Take Monty with you. He needs to lose some fat.' Cordelia shooed the pair of them towards the cloakroom. 'And wrap up well. There's a sharp wind.'

Ed put his arm round Issy's shoulders and gave her a squeeze.

'Come on. We'll go down to the farm and look at the chickens. They always cheer me up because they look ridiculous, clucking about the place. If you don't want to talk, that's fine. I can do silence. Monty,' he bellowed to the black-and-white spaniel sprawled in front of the Aga, 'walkies.'

He jangled the dog lead and, while Cordelia was sorting out a jacket and boots for Issy, clipped it onto Monty's collar.

'Best put this on too.' Cordelia rammed a bobble hat onto Issy's head. 'We don't want you getting earache. Now, Ed, look after Issy and bring her back in one piece.'

'Yes, ma'am.'

'I'm serious. I don't want any twisted ankles. Rabbit holes are dangerous things.'

Ed linked his arm through the crook of Issy's, and with Monty tugging at his lead they set off.

By the time they reached the stile that led to the far field, Issy's cheeks glowed from the effort of keeping up with Ed, and the physical activity gave her less time to brood about Don.

'What are you going to do now?' Ed

asked as Issy began to clamber over a rickety stile.

'At the present moment, my aim is to get over this thing safely.'

The stile rocked perilously as she attempted to gain a foothold. Ed moved in to steady it.

'Then what?'

'I suppose I've found out as much as I can about my mother.'

'What did Jonathan have to say?'

'There wasn't much he could tell me about Amy that I didn't already know. Like everyone else, he thought she was beautiful and harshly treated.'

'You're not thinking of going home?'

'There's nothing much to keep me here any more; apart from Bella, of course, although I don't know when I'll get to see her again.'

'And us,' Ed added in a quiet voice, 'the family; well, me in particular, actually.'

Issy's boots slipped on a slimy patch of damp moss sticking to the bar of the stile. Shrieking in shock she lashed out at Ed. Her face crashed into the cold zip of his wax jacket, the metal teeth digging into her cheek, causing her to cough violently as she inhaled the smell of dry caked mud.

'Shut up,' Ed bellowed to Monty as the dog ran round in excited circles, the tip of his tail hitting Issy's boots. 'Are you all right?'

'Think so,' Issy gasped.

'Can you sort out your legs,' Ed's breath was warm against Issy's ear as he held her steady, 'now Monty's stopped bashing your boots?'

With knees that threatened to buckle under her at any moment, Issy landed feet-first in the mud. Monty gave a quiet woof of approval and licked her hand with his warm tongue.

'Got your balance?' Ed asked.

His hair was plastered to his head in damp patches and, like Issy, he was breathing heavily. The collar of his jacket was turned up against the chill wind, but the look in his eyes was far from cold.

Issy twisted her fingers round a strand of wool dangling from the cuff of his jumper. She tugged and felt it unwind a bit more. Drops of mist on her eyelashes blurred her vision. She shivered but she felt hot.

'What did you mean by saying *and me, actually?*' she demanded, moving away from him.

'Would you like me to spell it out for you?' Ed's voice sounded as though it hurt him to speak.

He moved back in, closer. Issy swayed against him.

'You're going to have to because I don't think I understand you.'

'If you go back to Ireland I'll have no one to argue with.'

'That's not good enough.'

'It's the best I can do. I'm not very good at this sort of thing. Now, if you were a dodgy landlord or a dubious moneylender and I was waving a microphone under your nose and pursuing you down a back alleyway, I'd be singing like a canary.'

Beads of perspiration moistened Ed's brow and he was beginning to look uncomfortably warm.

'I'm going to need your help in this,' he admitted.

'You are on your own,' Issy responded, 'so get singing.'

'Can't you see how I feel about you — what are you looking at, and what's so funny?' Ed demanded, aware that he didn't have Issy's full attention.

'Do you know you cut yourself shaving this morning?' Issy enquired. 'There's a patch of dried blood under your left ear, and you've missed a bit of whisker, too.'

'Would you believe me if I said it was because I was in a hurry to see you again?' A questioning smile tugged the corner of Ed's mouth.

Issy shook her head slowly from side to side.

'I thought you wouldn't.'

Ed stroked Issy's nose with the tip of his gloved finger.

'What are you doing?'

'Trying to improve my lovemaking technique.'

'Well, don't. It makes me want to sneeze.' Issy's lips felt as though they were made of rubber tyres.

'It's the best I can do in a muddy field.'

'Then your technique has room for development.'

'I told you, I'm an amateur. Until now, I've steered clear of lasting personal relationships.'

'Do you really want me to stay?'

'Now you're getting the hang of it,' Ed looked at her with warm approval, 'and the next step is this — '

Ed crushed Issy's body against his. The sudden movement disturbed the nesting rooks. All Issy could feel was the pressure of his lips on hers. His powerful chest was a solid wall of support without which Issy suspected she wouldn't have been able to stand up.

'How dare you?' she protested.

'I'm not going to apologise. It's

something I've wanted to do for a long time.'

'You mean, when you're not challenging everything I do?'

'Indifference is the killer in any relationship, so they say, and I'm certainly not indifferent to you. When it comes to these things, nature doesn't always follow the rules.'

'You had no right to kiss me, and if you think I need a man to lean on, I don't.'

'In that case — ' Ed released his hold. Caught off-balance, Issy sank to her knees. 'You were saying?' His eyes were full of laughter as he looked down at her.

'That was a mean trick,' Issy screeched, sending the rooks into further trauma.

'I was merely taking you at your word,' Ed replied, looking infuriatingly calm.

Monty nudged Issy in her back, sensing a new game.

'Before Monty finishes off the job

and you wind up face-down in the mud, would you like me to help you up?'

Issy's knees were stuck fast in ground sodden by months of winter weather.

'Please,' she ground out through gritted teeth.

'You're no lightweight, are you?' Ed yanked Issy to her feet. 'It's all that chocolate you've been eating; and you've got dead leaves stuck to your hat. Here, let me sort you out.' She could feel the warmth of his breath on her face as he extricated the bits of twig dropped by the startled rooks. 'That's all I can do for the moment.' He stepped back to admire his handiwork. 'You wouldn't win first prize in any best-dressed awards, I'm afraid.'

'Neither would you,' Issy muttered, twisting a stray strand of wool between her fingers. 'Your jumper's coming undone.'

'Only because you're unravelling it.' Ed rammed her dislodged bobble hat back on her head.

Issy's face still flamed from the strength of his kiss. Through bruised lips she mumbled, 'You promised me a walk.'

'I did, didn't I?'

'I wasn't expecting extras.' Her eyes felt hot, but she resisted the urge to rest her head on Ed's broad shoulder.

'I know how devastated you must be feeling about Don,' the note of teasing was gone from his voice, 'and all that's happened; but I thought I might not get another chance to tell you how I feel. If you go back to Ireland, we may never see each other again. It was a case of now or never.'

'I can't talk about anything right now,' Issy insisted, still trying to control her raging senses.

'Understood, but promise you won't disappear on me without a word?'

Issy nodded. 'I promise.'

'Right. Let's go chat up the chickens.' Ed linked his fingers through hers. 'This way.'

The light was fading from the day by

the time they returned to Burton Abbots. As they trundled up the back lawn past the summerhouse, Cordelia waved at them through the kitchen window.

Ed pushed open the cloakroom door.

'Leave your boots here,' he said. 'No one bothers too much about a bit of mud in this part of the house. It would only be a waste of time. Let me take your coat.'

'Monty,' Cordelia called after the dog as he padded into the kitchen, 'what have you been doing? Your paws are filthy. Will someone please clean up the dog? I'm up to my ears in jacket potatoes.'

'Come here, you smelly mutt.' Issy heard Jonathan's voice and the pattering of paws on the floor. 'Goodness, have you been mudwrestling the chickens?'

Monty woofed and began panting heavily in reply.

'You have? Who won?' Jonathan laughed.

Issy smiled at her reflection in the mirror. This was how she had always imagined family life to be: slightly chaotic, but warm and welcoming. She did the best she could with her hair, and tried to repair the damage to her jeans — without much success.

As she pushed open the connecting door to the kitchen, Monty was now snoring in his basket, exhausted by the afternoon's activities.

'Hope you've worked up an appetite,' Cordelia greeted Issy as she padded through to the kitchen. 'I've done us girls a mountain of salad and enough baked beans to float a battleship.' She gave a little shriek as she took in Issy's dishevelled appearance.

'I sort of fell over,' Issy admitted with a shamefaced smile.

'I hold you to blame for this,' Cordelia scolded Ed. 'I told you to look after our guest, not drag her through the mud.'

'Would you like me to change before supper?' Issy volunteered.

'Heavens, no.' Cordelia lifted the lid off the baked beans and peered inside. 'We're doing casual tonight. Ed, stop hanging around making the place look untidy. Come and stir the beans for me.'

'Yes, aunty.'

'And don't call me that. You know I don't like it. Cordelia will do well enough.'

'Where would we be without your culinary prowess, Cordelia?' Ed delivered a kiss on his aunt's cheek. 'No one opens a tin of beans like you.'

She pushed him away with an indulgent smile. 'I can see your walk has done you good. Your cheeks are quite red too, Issy.' She looked hard at her. 'I hope my nephew hasn't been misbehaving himself by trying to kiss you? I've had to tell him about it before.'

Issy cast an uncomfortable glance in Ed's direction.

'I am only teasing, darling,' Cordelia laughed, but there was a twinkle in her eye. 'The men are watching the football. If you've finished ruining the beans, why don't you join them, Ed?'

'Sure you'll be OK?' he asked Issy. 'I'll stay with you if you'd prefer it.'

'We'll manage, now off you go. It's time for some girl talk.' Cordelia hustled him out of the kitchen. 'They'll be at it for hours. My two sons-in-law have arrived, but there's no sign of Penny or Sophie, so let's have a quiet drink on our own. I'll fetch a bottle from the fridge. The glasses are in the top cupboard. See what you can find.' She emerged a few moments later from the cold room. 'Here we are. I'm afraid it's only supermarket plonk. Jonathan won't let me near his vintage collection. He says I don't have a palate, whatever that is. He's probably right. All that nonsense about *I'm getting a taste of raspberries in aspic* is beyond me.' Cordelia uncorked the bottle and poured the white wine. 'Now: a toast. What do you suggest?'

Issy raised her glass.

'Thank you for inviting me this weekend,' she said.

'It's an absolute pleasure, darling. I'm afraid my girls are strong-willed, and we're always arguing. That's why they've taken themselves off. It's nice to have a friendly female to talk to. Sorry, I'm babbling, I know. Do you want to talk about Don Dealy, or is the subject a no-go area? I mean, tell me to shut up if you like.'

'I've only met him a couple of times,' Issy admitted.

'I've seen his show, of course; who hasn't? I can't really say it was my sort of thing, but it gave pleasure to a lot of people. He'll be sorely missed.'

Issy hesitated.

'Do you know about my background?' she asked Cordelia.

'Yes,' Cordelia replied in a soft voice.

'Your husband was on the prosecution team.'

'We never discussed his work. He liked to relax when he was at home, but the case was big news at the time.'

'I can't remember my mother, but everyone says she was beautiful.'

'The pictures I saw of her, she looked so fragile I wanted to give her a great big hug. When I think of what some people get away with, it was an absolute scandal the way she was treated.'

'Do you think she was guilty?'

Cordelia swallowed some wine.

'I don't know, but whatever she did I'm convinced she would have had her reasons,' Cordelia put down her glass and squeezed Issy's hand, 'and we are not here to judge her.'

Issy watched the bubbles in her wine glass rise to the top.

'Ed said much the same thing.'

'Do you want to look at the news?' Cordelia nodded towards the television set on the wall. 'I turned it off because they were going round in circles with their tributes to Don.'

'Perhaps later,' Issy replied.

The sound of laughter and more noise coming from the conservatory interrupted them. Monty woke, and with an excited bark jumped out of his basket and trotted across the room out into the hall, his tail wagging nineteen to the dozen.

'Looks like the girls are back. Come and meet them. Bring your drink.' Cordelia scooped up the bottle. 'Tell you what, why don't we hold a wake in Don's memory, our own little tribute?'

'He would have liked that,' Issy replied.

'Then come on.' Cordelia linked her arm through Issy's. 'Let's get the party started.'

18

'There you are, Issy,' the hotel receptionist greeted her like an old friend. 'We have a message for you.' She passed over her room key and a slip of paper.

'Who's it from?' Issy could feel Ed's warm breath on her cheek as he peered over her shoulder. 'Hey,' he protested as she moved away, 'we're partners, remember?' His fingers hovered over hers, ready to snatch the slip of paper out of her grasp.

Issy hesitated. Since Ed had kissed her in that muddy field she had felt things were moving too fast between them. He hadn't made any reference to it for the rest of the weekend, but its shadow hovered between them.

'Coffee in the bar?' she suggested, reluctant to invite him up to her room.

'Want anything to eat?' Ed asked as he picked up the menu.

Issy shook her head. 'I couldn't. Cordelia has to be one of the most generous hostesses in Gloucestershire.'

Penny and Sophie had proved as vibrant as their mother and were clearly delighted to be introduced to Issy. It was as Issy had feared: they assumed she was Ed's latest female companion. Ed did nothing to dispel their suspicions.

'Have you told Issy about our night of passion in the summerhouse?' Penny teased Ed with an arch smile in Issy's direction.

'Was that when you were two-timing your current boyfriend before you ditched them both and went off backpacking to South America?' Issy had enquired with an equally teasing smile.

Ed burst into laughter as surprise spread across Penny's face.

'You'll have to do some quick thinking to explain that one to your husband,' he said before Penny hurriedly changed the subject.

The rest of the weekend passed without incident. After their baked potato supper Cordelia hustled Issy and Ed into the study and whispered, 'If you want to look at the news, feel free. I'll make sure you're not disturbed.'

They had sat together on a rickety old sofa, Ed clutching Issy's hand in a sympathetic gesture of support. Monty had padded into the room and slumped down onto her feet. The heat from his body warmed her toes.

'We'd best get it over with,' Ed said, his brown eyes softened by the low table lamps Cordelia had turned on for them.

Issy was having more and more difficulty ignoring his quiet message of love. She wanted to believe in his feelings for her, but she couldn't forget he was a journalist and no stranger to human drama. Recently so many people had let her down, and she was beginning to doubt her own confidence. For all she knew, Ed could be using her as a career opportunity, and once her celebrity status was spent he would ditch her.

The news item reported that Don had complained of feeling unwell during filming and his agent had called for an ambulance. Flowers had been placed on the railings outside the hospital once the news had broken.

Issy had not wanted to dwell on further details. 'I've seen enough,' she said, and Ed turned the set off.

'Do you feel up to joining the others?' he asked. 'There'll probably be a lot of silliness going on.'

'That sounds exactly what I need.' Issy replied.

The remainder of the evening had passed in playing mindless board games, during which a lot of good-natured cheating went on. Monty appeared to have adopted Issy as his for the evening and, along with Ed, hardly left her side.

Now, after the long drive back to the hotel, Ed eased down into one of the deep leather chairs while they waited for their coffee to arrive.

'Who's the message from?' he asked.

Issy unfolded her note.

'Lucinda Whitby. She wants me to ring her.'

Ed and Issy looked at each other in surprise.

'Do you think she blames me for what happened?' Issy had difficulty swallowing.

'There's only one way to find out,' Ed replied.

With her heartbeat thudding in her ears Issy punched in the number Lucinda had given her. It rang for a long time before Lucinda answered.

'It's Issy,' she said.

'I left a message for you, didn't I?' Lucinda sounded vague.

'I'm so sorry about Don.'

'The funeral is the day after tomorrow, family only.'

'I understand,' Issy replied. 'I've no intention of gatecrashing.'

'I would like you to be there.'

'Sorry?' Issy wasn't sure she had

heard Lucinda properly.

'Come to the main house.'

The line went dead.

'Well?' Ed demanded.

'Lucinda wants me to go to Don's funeral.' Issy repeated Lucinda's request.

'I'll drive you down,' Ed insisted.

'It's a private service. Why does she want me there?'

'Perhaps it was Don's request.' Ed picked up a newspaper. There were pictures of Don all over the front page. 'The service is at eleven o'clock. I'll be here in good time,' he promised.

* * *

Ed was wearing a dark suit and a tie. He peered at Issy under the brim of the black hat she had borrowed from one of the girls on reception.

'OK?' he queried, his face full of concern.

'I haven't slept very well,' Issy admitted.

'Did you have any breakfast?'

'A slice of toast and some coffee.'

'Sure that's enough?'

'Don't fuss, please.' Issy picked at her black gloves.

'Anything you say. Make yourself comfortable and we'll be off.'

Issy sank into the welcome warmth of the saloon car, closed her eyes and let the motion of the car lull her to sleep.

She felt a gentle touch on her arm.

'We're nearly there,' Ed said.

He was navigating the tortuous lane that led to Swallow House.

'I put your hat on the back seat. You were in danger of crushing it.' Ed cast her a sideways glance. 'I also turned up the heating. Feeling better?'

Issy stretched out her cramped legs and arched her back.

'I think so,' she replied, doing her best to ignore the tight ball of tension knotting her stomach.

'Look.' Ed pointed to a clump of bright orange crocuses nestling in the grass on the verge at the side of road.

He drew over into a small layby. 'Would you like some? Wait here.'

Issy watched as he bent down and parted the grass to reveal another clump of purple, white and yellow buds. Clutching the small bouquet he made his way back to the car.

'I think I saw a rubber band and some tissues in the glove compartment.' He reached across and, rummaging around, found what he wanted and secured the stalks with a blue band before wrapping them in pink tissues. 'There.' He handed them over. 'Something to cheer you up. Now,' he glanced at his watch 'best be on our way. It wouldn't do to be late.'

Cars were double-parked down the drive as Ed approached the house.

'What are you going to do?' Issy asked as she opened the passenger door.

'I've one or two contacts in the area. I'll touch base with them and see what's going on. You've got my mobile number?'

He touched her cheek with his hand. Issy was glad the brim of her hat shielded her eyes.

'I'll call you when I'm through,' she said.

'Any time,' he said before he drove off.

Issy's hand hovered over the carved bullfrog doorknocker, but before she could raise it Mrs Hammond opened the door. The housekeeper was dressed in black and her eyes were red-rimmed.

'Oh, miss, it's good to see you.'

To Issy's surprise, the housekeeper hugged her warmly and kissed her on the cheek.

'The family are in the conservatory.'

Issy's footsteps echoed down the deserted hall. The air was redolent with the warm smell of beeswax.

Lucinda, a pale figure in a black dress, was seated on one of the cushioned wicker chairs. Small groups of people were hovering around her, chatting in quiet voices. Several curious glances were cast in her direction as

Issy hovered in the doorway, uncertain what to do next.

'It's Issy Dillaine, isn't it?' a grey haired man murmured in her ear. 'I'm Tom, Don's agent, an honorary member of the family. You won't remember me, but I was a guest the first time you visited Swallow House.'

'I don't really know why I'm here,' Issy replied in a low voice.

'I'm sure Lucinda will explain,' he replied and drifted away.

'How kind,' Lucinda said as Issy offered her the bunch of wayside flowers Ed had picked a few moments earlier.

'Would you like me to put them in water for you?' a hovering woman asked.

'No. Issy gave them to me.' Lucinda clutched the flowers to her chest. 'I'll take them with me to the church.'

'I understand you'll be travelling with Mrs Dealy?' A dark-suited man approached Issy.

'Am I?' She turned to face him.

'If you'll come with me, one of my colleagues will attend to Mrs Dealy.'

More perplexed than ever, Issy sat in the back seat of the limousine. Lucinda didn't speak, but squeezed Issy's hand tightly during the short drive to the church.

A small crowd had gathered outside; but, respecting Lucinda's request for privacy, the press had stayed away.

The service was simple and soon over.

'There's to be a memorial service later,' Tom informed Issy as everyone stood around outside the church. At Lucinda's request hers had been the only floral tribute, but in a touching gesture of condolence she had placed Issy's small bunch of crocuses next to it.

'Are you coming back to Swallow House?' Tom asked.

'My friend is waiting for me,' Issy replied; now her duty was done, she was keen to leave the churchyard as soon as decently possible. She still had no idea why Lucinda had requested she attend the service. Apart from Tom, no-one had spoken to her.

Lucinda finished talking to the vicar and walked towards Issy.

'I didn't allow you more time together with Don,' she apologised. 'I should have done. It was mean of me. Is it too late to say I'm sorry for the way I've behaved towards you?'

A middle-aged woman approached them and cast Issy an unfriendly look.

'I think we should be getting back to Swallow House, Aunt Lucinda.'

'A moment, please.' Lucinda held up a hand.

'Don't tire her out,' the woman hissed at Issy, 'she's been through enough.'

'I have something for you,' Lucinda said, searching in her capacious black bag.

She produced a stiff white envelope and handed it over. Issy's name had been written in flamboyant script on the front in the bold blue fountain-pen ink she knew Don favoured.

'It explains everything.' Lucinda patted her hand. 'I'm sorry,' she repeated.

'We really do have to leave, Aunt Lucinda.' Her niece was back by her side. 'You'll catch a chill hanging around this draughty churchyard.'

Without a glance in Issy's direction she ushered Lucinda to the waiting car. Its engine was already running and Issy watched the pair of them climb into the back seat. With a gentle purr of increased power, the car eased away from the lych gate, leaving Issy alone in the windswept churchyard.

'The church is still open,' the vicar smiled, 'if you would like a few quiet moments to reflect? You won't be disturbed.'

Thanking him, Issy went back inside, her footsteps echoing on the stone flooring.

Bright sunlight reflected through the stained glass windows, creating a kaleidoscope of colour on the polished pews that smelt of lavender and lilies. Issy pushed aside one of the hand-embroidered hassocks and sat down.

With trembling fingers she slit open the envelope and extracted a sheet of expensive notepaper. She closed her eyes for a few moments to relax her racing heartbeat; then, taking a deep breath, she began to read Don's letter.

My Dear Issy,

When I saw you on that rocking horse the night we first met, you took my breath away. You were so like your mother. You have her hair and eyes and the same smile.

I'm so glad you came back into our lives even though our time together was short.

I have made arrangements for you to continue to receive your allowance. Please don't do anything noble like refusing to accept it. It's yours to do with as you wish. Lucinda and I have no children. You are the closest we came to having a child, and we both want you to lead a happy and fulfilled life.

As you're reading this, I presume the doctors were right to tell me to slow down, but I've never been one to take things easy. I've always lived life to the full.

I wish we could have got to know each other better, but perhaps it's for the best. On further acquaintance you would have found faults in me. I've got plenty; but you, my sweet girl, are perfect in every way.

Raise a glass in my memory from time to time, and remember Amy would want you to enjoy your life.

With every ounce of my love,
Don

Issy refolded Don's letter and placed it carefully in her bag. Lucinda was wrong. Don's letter explained nothing at all.

19

Ed took one look at Issy, a forlorn figure in a too-big black hat standing by the weather-beaten gravestones, and leapt out of the driver's seat of his car. Her shoulders trembled under his touch as he put his arm round her. 'Here.' He produced a hip flask from the pocket of his coat and guided it to her lips. 'Take a sip. Steady,' he added, as whisky threatened to spill down her dress.

She spluttered, clearing her throat.

'Get in the car. The heater's going at full blast — and take that wretched thing off.' He tossed her hat onto the back seat.

Ed began to reverse the car back up the twisty lane. Issy massaged her numbed legs with fingers that were stiff and wouldn't work properly. Her breath came in short sharp bursts.

'Th- . . . thank you,' she stuttered.

'What did they do to you?' he demanded.

'Nothing,' Issy insisted. 'I'm fine.'

'You're spending the night at my place, and I'm not taking no for an answer.'

The whisky began to warm Issy's toes and her fingers tingled back to life.

'Not tonight, Ed,' she said in a raspy voice. 'I can't.'

'You're not going back to your hotel,' he said in a firm voice. 'Subject closed.'

Issy let out a sigh of submission, grateful that the decision had been taken out of her hands.

'Then I give in.'

'That's more like it.' Ed nodded approval. 'Now . . . ' He straightened the car as they reached the top of the lane. 'Let's put some rubber on the road.'

He swerved to avoid a traffic cone and, easing up a gear, drove off.

'How was Lucinda?' he asked as the car settled down.

'Composed, dignified.' Issy shook her head. 'Odd.'

'Was she pleased to see you?' Ed persisted.

'We travelled together to the church and she held my hand so tightly I got cramp. She put my little bunch of flowers next to her wreath.'

'Sounds like you did a great job comforting her, but you're right: that was odd behaviour,' Ed acknowledged.

'There was some sort of niece who carried on the family tradition of being unwelcoming.' Issy gave a brief smile. 'She tried to get Lucinda away from me as soon as she could.'

'And they didn't invite you back to Swallow House? They drove off and left you in the churchyard? Nice one.'

'Lucinda gave me a letter from Don. The vicar let me read it in the church.'

'At least someone showed some compassion. Are you going to tell me what it said?' Ed prompted when Issy lapsed back into silence.

'Don was the person responsible for

paying my monthly allowance.'

Ed banged the steering wheel.

'So it was him all along?'

'He's made arrangements for his estate to continue paying it. He said it was with Lucinda's blessing.'

Ed eyebrows met his floppy fringe.

'There's a turn-up for the books.'

'I don't know that I should accept it, although he wants me to.'

'You don't have to think about it now. Was there anything else?'

'Why would he have set up that account in the first place, and also want the estate to start paying it again?'

'Perhaps he had a guilty conscience over what happened between him and Finlay, Lucinda's brother.'

'What did happen?'

'There was a boating accident.'

'I know, but that was nothing to do with my mother.'

'I'm not so sure. I think there was more between Amy and Finlay than we realised, and it would explain why Lucinda wasn't too friendly when you

244

first met her. Her baby brother was the apple of her eye.'

'How do you know?'

'Those people I met up with today?' Ed said slowly. 'One of them was doing a tribute to Don. He's a journalist of the old school and always checks everything three times.'

Ed cast her Issy a sideways glance.

'The smart money says Finlay was your father.'

'Lucinda's brother?'

'Right. She doted on him, then your mother comes along and suddenly Lucinda's not numero uno in his life any more. It was a bitter pill to swallow.'

'Did Finlay know about me?'

'I've no idea, but perhaps Don suspected? Maybe Lucinda saw a resemblance to her brother in you? Who knows?'

'And that's why I was invited to the funeral today? Because I am part of the family?'

'You're Lucinda's niece.'

'Then Don Dealy was my uncle?'

'By marriage, yes.' Ed hesitated. 'There's something else.'

'What?'

'I don't know how to tell you, but your cover's been blown.'

'What do you mean?'

'There hasn't been a moment of Don's life that hasn't come under the microscope. For a while, Amy Grant was a big part of his life. My uncle wasn't the only one to pick up on your ad in the personal column. Other people saw it and probably worked out the connection.'

'I didn't say I was Amy's daughter.'

'You didn't have to. It hasn't taken the press long to work out the relationship, and they are on your case.'

'What am I going to do?' Issy asked, appalled at the thought of her privacy being invaded.

'There's no need to panic. Not many people can positively identify you. The press stayed away from the funeral at Lucinda's request. The only people who know who you are for certain are Roger

Street and Lucinda, and they will, I think, want to keep a low profile.'

'What about your family?'

'You can rely on them to be discreet. No worries there.'

'We've forgotten Harry Willetts. He knows.'

'You're right. He's someone we'll have to keep an eye out for. He may not want to publicise his part in Roger's plan of pretending to be his brother, but you never know. The media exposure would promote his flagging career.'

'You've no idea where he is, I suppose?' Issy asked.

'None at all.'

'I haven't seen him for ages,' Issy said.

'Like everyone else in this affair, he's probably gone to ground. But if you get any more letters in reply to your advert, don't answer them.'

Issy stifled a yawn of exhaustion.

'I presume you've heard nothing from Roger Street?' Ed asked.

She shook her head.

'Something tells me we won't.'

'Poor Amy,' Issy reflected. 'I can't help feeling she was the victim in all this.'

'Don must have been torn in all directions. His priority was obviously Lucinda, but he must have felt responsible for Amy and you.'

'Do you really think Lucinda suspected I might be Finlay's daughter?'

Ed concentrated on a tricky bit of motorway for a few moments, negotiating another hazard in the road.

'I heard from an unofficial source that Don and Lucinda wanted to adopt you.'

Issy cast her mind back to the night she'd first met Don and Lucinda in the nursery in Swallow House. Had the rocking horse been meant for her? Was that why she had felt so happy with the books and the farmyard and the little train set?

'What went wrong?' Issy asked.

'I don't know for sure; it might have

been Lucinda's fragile health. But for some reason your mother made arrangements to go to Ireland, and that was that.'

'If Lucinda loved her brother as much as you say she did, why was she so unwelcoming to me?'

'It's only a theory on my part, but . . . The one thing everyone agrees on is that you look like your mother?'

'Yes,' Issy agreed.

'Every time Lucinda looked at you, she saw Amy. In her eyes, you were a constant reminder of the woman who had ruined her life.'

'Why did Amy never tell anyone?'

'As I said, it's possible Don did know.'

'Didn't I have a right to know as well?'

'It's possible your adopted parents knew too. From what you've told me, they were quite good at keeping things secret.'

Issy closed her eyes and leaned back in her seat. What a shock she must have given Lucinda when she saw her riding that rocking horse. Issy couldn't help wondering how very different her life would have been had Don and Lucinda succeeded in adopting her.

A jet destined for City Airport flew overhead. Dark business buildings were etched in a dramatic silhouette against the night sky. It was all so very different from where Issy had grown up. City life wasn't for her. She missed the sound of the sea and purple sunsets. She even missed the soft rain and misty mornings and the smell of peat. No one knew who you were in London. Back home, everyone greeted you by name.

Ed drew up outside the converted warehouse.

'Here we are.'

'I feel like I want to sleep for a hundred years,' Issy said.

'In that case,' Ed replied, 'leave everything to me. I've a bottle of red upstairs. A hot bath awaits, and then I prescribe my sauce Edouard and an early night. How does that sound?'

'Magic.' Issy smiled at him.

'You can have my bed. I'll shake down on the sofa — if I can work out how to get the wretched thing open without losing a finger.'

Issy's lips trembled into a faint smile.

'Do you have anything to go with your sauce Edouard?'

'I'm tempted to say 'me'; but that's not the answer you're looking for, is it?'

Issy shook her head.

'I do have some interestingly-shaped pasta in the cupboard. So, if you're ready . . . ? Don't forget your hat.' Ed picked it up off the back seat. 'We don't want squirrels nesting in it overnight.'

'You have wildlife round here?'

'You'd be surprised at what goes on after midnight.'

He grabbed her hand and entwined his fingers between hers. They were warm to the touch, and Issy's weakened resolve was on the verge of collapse.

'I need overnight things,' she managed to say in a steady voice.

'I think I can accommodate you on

that one. Penny stayed over a while ago before flying off somewhere early the next morning. She left some stuff behind. I'm sure she won't mind if you borrow something of hers.'

'Why didn't she stay in Jonathan's flat?' Issy demanded.

'Because he was staying there with Cordelia, and you know how Penny and her mother rub each other up the wrong way. If you don't believe me, you can ring Penny up and ask her. I'll give you her number. Do you want it?'

'Guess I've got used to doubting everyone,' Issy apologised.

'Then you'll have to learn to trust again, won't you?' Ed unlocked his front door. 'You've been living too long in the shadows.'

It was warm and snug inside the warehouse. Ed switched on the lighting and, tugging at his tie, eased it away from his shirt collar and undid the top button.

'*Now* what have I done?' he demanded as Issy stared at him.

'I'm not sure,' she said slowly, 'but I think I'd like you to kiss me.'

'In that case,' Ed advanced slowly towards her, 'supper may be slightly delayed.'

In the distance a boat hooted on the river.

'Do you think the skipper's issuing a hazard warning?' Issy's breath came in short bursts.

'Too late, I'd say, wouldn't you?' Ed said. 'Much too late.'

20

'Are you hungry?' Ed asked as morning sunlight filtered through the blinds.

'Mm,' came the lazy response from the bed.

'Get up, you lazy thing.'

'It's early.'

'I don't care. My back's aching. I didn't sleep a wink on that wretched sofa. The manufacturers should be sued, saying it offers a comfortable night's sleep. It does no such thing.'

'Stop grumbling — and don't do that!'

Ed had been tugging at the duvet in an attempt to get Issy to open her eyes.

'My memory's a bit hazy on the subject, but I think you fell asleep on me and we never did get round to eating supper.'

'We didn't,' Issy murmured.

'You do realise you are totally responsible for curdling my Sauce Edouard?'

'We could try eating it for breakfast,'
Issy suggested.

'What a disgusting thought.' Ed
shuddered.

Issy stretched out her legs and smiled
up at him.

'You resemble a cat that's got the
cream.'

'I am starved. So, if Sauce Edouard is
off the menu, what's for breakfast?'

'I suppose you don't fancy a glass of
red wine?' Ed caught the look on Issy's
face. 'Thought you wouldn't. Then I
have to break it to you, I don't think
there's much else in the house.'

Ed opened a drawer, then pulled a
t-shirt over his head before searching
around for his shoes.

'What are you doing?'

'I'm off to the corner bakery for
supplies. You make the coffee. I'll be
back in fifteen minutes.'

Issy heard the door bang behind
him. Shrugging on Penny's silk

dressing-gown, she padded towards the kitchenette. The sun dazzled the water. She slid open the window and took a deep breath of early-morning air. It felt clean and fresh and cleansed her lungs.

Turning back to the worktop, she scooped coffee into the pot and inhaled the aroma of roasted beans as the liquid began to bubble up. Leaving it to percolate, she headed for the shower. By the time she emerged dressed in jeans and one of Penny's shirts, Ed was back with a paper bag bulging with goodies.

'I got croissants, a walnut-and-date Danish and a double-ended yellow.'

'A what?'

'I've no idea of the correct technical term, but it's got yellow confectioner's custard oozing out of each end and is to die for.' He nudged the plate of pastries at her. 'Enjoy while I grab a shower; that is, if you've left any hot water.'

Issy rubbed at her damp hair with a spare towel, then poured out a mug of coffee and began to nibble on a flaky almond croissant. Traffic on the river was building up and she watched a tourist boat full of excited trippers cruise by. She stifled a lazy yawn.

Ed emerged from the shower and, following her example, helped himself to coffee and a Danish pastry. His hair was still mussed from where he hadn't combed it properly.

'Do you normally eat breakfast at this time of the morning?' Issy demanded.

'It depends on what I've been up to the night before.' Ed began to smear apricot jam on a croissant. 'Once we've recharged our batteries I foresee a long, lazy day in front of us. How 'bout the newspapers and some trashy TV — what's wrong?' he asked as Issy's smile faltered.

'I have to go back home,' she said.

'Not right now?' Ed protested.

'Soon.'

Ed dropped his croissant back onto his plate. 'What's brought this on?'

'You asked me not to run out on you,

and I'm not, but we can't carry on like this.'

'What do you mean?'

'Whatever we had between us is over.'

'Well, thanks for breaking the news to my face and not disappearing without a word. I have to hand it to you for style.'

'You do understand, don't you?' Issy pleaded.

'No, I don't.'

'We have no future together. We live in different countries. I'm the daughter of a woman with a dubious past. Do I have to go on?'

Ed's happy smile had now been replaced by a look of disbelief.

'I think you're going to have to come up with something better than that.'

'I have commitments.' Issy was clutching her mug of coffee so tightly her fingers hurt.

'You have commitments here. There's your grandmother — sorry, step-grandmother. Are you intending to walk out on her too?'

Issy pushed away the remains of her uneaten breakfast.

'This isn't easy for me.'

'How do you think I feel?' Ed was now flushed with anger. 'We've been through so much together.'

'I know, but it isn't that simple.'

'I had you figured all wrong. Serves me right, I suppose, for breaking my own rule of never believing a word anyone says. I've been sold some pretty convincing stories in my time, but you take the gold star.'

'Don't make things worse,' Issy pleaded.

'Tell me, do you make a habit of this? Ditching guys once they've outlived their usefulness?'

'That's an outrageous thing to say!'

It was a few moments before Ed could control his breathing enough to speak again.

'You're right. I think I'd better drive you back to your hotel.'

'Ed, listen to me.'

He shook her hand off his arm.

'You've said enough. I get the picture. I am yesterday. I'll fetch the car.'

* * *

Ed drew up outside the hotel. Neither of them had spoken a word during the journey.

'I'll launder Penny's things and send them back to you,' Issy said.

'Please yourself,' was Ed's terse reply before he drove off, not bothering to look at her or wave goodbye.

Issy stood disconsolately on the pavement, watching his car turn the corner and disappear from sight. He hadn't suggested keeping in touch, and in her heart of hearts Issy knew it was for the best if they didn't see each other again. Falling in love had been the last thing she had meant to do; and she certainly hadn't expected to find love with the nephew of the man who had in part been responsible for prosecuting her mother.

260

She turned towards the swing doors and, with her vision blurred, made her way into the hotel foyer.

'We thought you might be staying overnight with Lucinda Whitby,' the receptionist greeted Issy, 'after the funeral.'

Issy hoped the flush staining her cheeks wasn't too tell-tale.

'Thank you.' She accepted her room key. 'I'm sorry I didn't telephone. It slipped my mind.'

'No worries.' The receptionist turned back to the pigeonhole. 'This came for you.' She passed over a large buff-coloured envelope.

'Can you make up my bill?' Issy asked.

'You're checking out?'

'As soon as I can arrange a flight home.'

'Is this because of the newspapers?' the receptionist asked.

'Sorry?'

The receptionist lowered her voice and produced a tabloid from under the desk and tapped a picture on the front page with her fingernail. 'Isn't that Harry Willetts?'

Harry's handsome face smiled out at her from underneath an exclusive banner. Issy gulped as she read the lurid headlines.

'*My Time With Amy Grant's Daughter.*' There was a blurred picture of Issy that looked as though it had been taken on a mobile phone and in a hurry. She stared aghast at the article. It was as she and Ed had feared. Harry had sold his story to the press.

'I don't want any calls.' Issy scrunched up the newspaper.

'I understand,' the receptionist replied with a sympathetic look. 'I'll make sure you're not bothered

Clutching her envelope, Issy rode up to her floor in the lift. She had made the right decision to go home. There was nothing more she could do here.

The fuss would soon die down. Ed would be off around the world on another assignment and Issy would go back to her job in Cork, and life would settle back into normal day-to-day routine.

Issy tossed the buff envelope onto her bed and opened the wardrobe doors. It didn't take her long to pack, and the room sounded hollow after she'd emptied the dressing table and taken her things out of the wardrobe.

She sat on the bed and dragged her mobile out of her bag. There were several missed calls from numbers she couldn't identify. She ignored them.

The caller identification flashed up Jonathan Jackson's number as the phone began to ring.

'Issy?' His reassuring voice came down the line. 'How are you bearing up?'

'I'm fine.'

'Have you seen today's papers?'

'Only the headlines.'

'Then keep it that way. Harry's really gone to town. His story is so full of inaccuracies it's laughable. Cordelia is incandescent, and threatening to come down to London and personally throttle him.'

'That's kind of her.' Issy felt a warm glow in the pit of her stomach. It was nice to know how much she cared. 'But Harry's disappeared.'

'Good riddance. Anyway, the reason I telephoned is because I thought you should know there's a warrant out for Roger Street's arrest.'

'What?'

'New evidence has come to light.'

'After all this time?'

'The police have received a document implicating him in the scandal. It names people, places and dates; and, what's more, it's in Roger's handwriting.'

'How do you know?' Issy gasped.

'Apparently it's been verified by an expert. One of my old contacts has been in touch.'

'Do you have any idea where it came from?'

'Bella Tucker. Isn't she the woman who married your grandfather?'

'What?'

'You understand this is unofficial?'

'Go on,' Issy urged.

'The story goes she found it in an old suitcase in an envelope. It was addressed to Bella but was unopened. Robbie Tucker had signed the seal on the back. It was filed away with Amy's other bits and pieces.'

'And for all these years it's been hidden in a suitcase?'

'And everyone forgot about it.'

'I think Robbie was probably protecting Bella's interests. She told me how annoyed he used to get when Amy upset her and how he would try to keep them apart, but I wonder how the documents came into Amy's possession in the first place.'

'I have no idea, and now we shall never know,' Jonathan said with a tinge of sadness in his voice.

'Amy must have sent them to Bella for safekeeping. Perhaps she too forgot about them. You're sure the notes are genuine?' Issy asked.

'Genuine enough to convince the authorities.'

'That must have been what Roger Street was looking for,' Issy mused, 'and why he set up Harry to keep tabs on me.'

'You will keep in touch, won't you? I know Cordelia and the girls would love to meet up again.'

Assuring Jonathan she would do her best, Issy rang off. But keeping in touch with him and his family would mean explanations about Ed, and right now she wasn't sure she was up to it.

Issy stretched out on the bed and tried to think things through. Had Amy's numbers-dyslexia prevented her from realising the importance of the document she held? Did she even know it was in her possession? If she didn't, it would explain why she hadn't mentioned it to the authorities.

As Issy shifted position on the bed, she rolled onto the envelope the desk receptionist had given her. She tugged it free. It wasn't sealed, and a black-and-white photograph slid onto the bedcover.

Issy turned it over. It was of her mother arm in arm with a man. They were both sporting buttonholes, standing under a lych gate and smiling brightly for the camera. Amy was wearing a two-piece suit with a matching petal hat. On the back was written the words: *Amy and Finlay on their wedding day.*

This further discovery proved too much for Issy's self-control. Tears slid down her cheeks. The photograph confirmed Finlay was her father. Issy's vision blurred as she looked at the two of them united in love.

There was no date, but the warden Sally Fay had attached a sticky note underneath the caption informing Issy that Bella had finally gone through her suitcase of old photos, where they had come across this one. Issy inspected it again. She could see Finlay's resemblance to Lucinda, the tilt of his head and the faint air of superiority.

Issy now knew for certain it had been her parents' presence she had felt that first evening in the Swallow House nursery. Her actions had somehow created a private family time warp when, for a brief moment, the three of them had been together again and the room had been filled with their love for her.

She replaced the photograph in the envelope. Her story was over. It was time to go home.

21

The aircraft droned a comfortable mid-flight engine noise. The steward approached with a tray of drinks.

'Is there anything else I can get you, madam?' she asked when Issy shook her head.

'Do you know how long it will be before we land?'

'We have a strong tailwind so we're making good time, and we hope to be on schedule.'

Issy leaned back in her seat and closed her eyes. Ed's image kept floating into her mind's eye, making it impossible to relax. He was smiling that engaging crooked smile of his, and his hair was sticking out at a silly angle. Issy clenched the armrest, her knuckles taut. She had made the right decision. Her future and Ed's were destined to go in completely different directions.

She didn't want to make her parents' mistake of going through a wedding ceremony, only to risk being cruelly torn apart.

Before she had left, Issy had made a swift telephone call to Sally Fay to thank her for the photo of her parents and to pass on her love to Bella. Issy assured Sally she would visit again as soon as she could, and that she would be keeping in constant video-link touch now that a new activities organiser had been appointed.

'Our residents adore technology,' Sally Fay informed Issy, 'so any time, just log on.'

The call to Lucinda had been more difficult to make.

'I understand,' she said quietly when Issy explained that she was going home and probably wouldn't be back for a while.

She was looking at the picture of herself with her parents and wondering how to break the news of their marriage to Lucinda.

'I know Don arranged with his bank to set up an allowance for you, Issy — please don't interrupt.' There was a trace of the old Lucinda in her voice as she went on, 'He knew your mother and my brother were very close. I'm sorry for the things I said to you. If things had been different, maybe we could all have enjoyed a better relationship.'

'Lucinda,' Issy raised her voice, anxious to stem the older woman's flow, 'there's something I have to tell you.'

'The boating accident on the lake wasn't Amy's fault, although she and Finlay had had an argument. I expect it was about money. Finlay always over-spent, and I did wonder if he tried to persuade Amy to accept Roger's pro-posal to sell on any confidential details that came into her possession.'

'Lucinda, listen to me. I would have preferred to break the news to you in person, but I don't want you hearing it from anyone else.'

'What news?' Lucinda asked.

'I've received a photograph from my step-grandmother. It's of Finlay and my mother together.'

'I'd like to see it some time.'

Issy took a deep breath. 'It was taken on their wedding day.' She gritted her teeth and waited for Lucinda's reaction.

'Did you say wedding day?' she asked after a long pause.

'Finlay and my mother were married.'

'No. That's not true. Finlay would have told me.'

Issy chose her next words carefully.

'It's genuine.'

'Why didn't they tell me?' Lucinda sounded as though her words were being torn from her.

'Perhaps they were going to when the time was right.'

'If only Don hadn't washed his hands of Finlay . . . but he'd bailed out my brother so many times, he'd had enough. Though Finlay really was trying to turn over a new leaf. He must have loved Amy very much to marry her.'

'I'm sorry,' was all Issy could think of to say.

'Why was the photograph hidden away for so long?' Lucinda's voice was full of anguish.

'Bella didn't know she had it. Her relationship with Amy was always fragile. We think Bella's second husband Robbie put her things in a suitcase and locked them away.'

'When were they married — Finlay and Amy, I mean?'

'There's no date.'

'All this time and nobody knew.'

'Lucinda, I've been thinking,' Issy began. 'About the trust fund Don set up ... could we use it to create a performing arts scholarship in Don's memory?'

'It would mean a lot of work.'

'Yes, but do you think it's possible?'

'Of course it's possible.'

'Would you like to head it up?'

'That's very generous of you.'

'Why don't you come over to Ireland for a holiday? We could talk things through.'

'Are you sure?'

'Absolutely,' Issy insisted.

'In that case I'd like to very much,' Lucinda replied. 'And thank you.'

'Come as soon as you can,' Issy said before she rang off.

After she had made her call, an online check had revealed there was availability on the early evening flight to Cork, and Issy booked a window seat with an adjacent vacant aisle seat.

Her stomach had churned as she looked at the departure board, waiting for her gate to come up. The only person she hadn't said goodbye to was Ed. A part of her hoped he would come running through the glass doors at the last moment and beg her not to go; but she knew she was fantasising, and that sort of thing only happened in the movies as the closing credits were rolling. This wasn't the movies; this was real life.

Even so, the smell of percolating coffee would always remind her of the early-morning sun glinting on the river.

The departure board indicated her flight was ready to board. Issy gathered up her bags and headed towards the security controls.

And now, through the cabin window, the sun was painting the aircraft wingtips a rosy shade of pink. In the distance she could see a cloud covering the Emerald Isle. Soon they would begin their descent.

'Is this seat taken?'

Issy continued to look out of the window.

'Yes,' she fibbed. There was a disturbance in the adjacent seat as the newcomer ignored her rebuff and settled down beside her. She turned in annoyance.

Her eyes widened in shock. 'What are you doing here?' she demanded.

'Trying stay out of your way,' Ed replied, 'until it was too late for you to get off the plane. I had to fork out for a club-class seat. It was the only way I could do it.'

'Do what?'

'I think the crew suspect I am up to no good; so if things look a bit sticky, you *will* tell them I am who I say I am, and not a stalker, won't you?'

'Where did you come from?'

'I sneaked through that curtain there.' Ed pointed to the club class cabin. 'There was always the chance you might have spotted me through the chink in the curtain, so I've been hiding my face behind a newspaper for the past half hour, then I went to the washroom for a bit while I plucked up the courage to confront you. I'm not cut out to be a spook.'

Ed squeezed Issy's fingers, his face alight as he recounted his adventure.

'How did you know I was on this flight?'

'I bribed that nice receptionist at your hotel. I told her it was a matter of life and death. Corny, I know, but it worked. Time was pretty tight and I nearly missed the flight. A friend gave me a lift to the airport on the back of his motorbike. It was a pretty hairy journey, I can tell you. I've got one of those express cards that let you board after the flight's officially closed. You're only supposed to use it for business reasons, but after I'd catapulted myself through the doors and exercised my charm on the check-in girls, they let me through.'

'Is this passenger bothering you, madam?' a female steward approached.

'Yes he is,' Issy replied in a loud voice.

Several heads turned in their direction.

'In that case, sir, would you mind returning to your correct seat?'

'Issy,' Ed implored, 'this isn't funny. Tell her who I am.'

Sensing disruption, a male steward approached.

'If you don't do as we ask, sir, I'll be forced to call the captain.'

'Good idea,' Ed enthused. 'He can

marry us, can't he? Or is that only on a ship?'

The male steward stared hard at Ed.

'Aren't you that reporter who does all those in-depth exposures?

'If I say yes, will you let me stay?' Ed implored. 'This lady is wanted for questioning,' he added.

Issy could now feel all eyes were on her.

'I haven't done anything wrong,' she insisted.

'Tell them about the case.' Ed nudged Issy with his elbow. 'My uncle was part of the prosecuting team,' he informed the two stewards. 'That's how we met. Didn't you read about it in the press?'

'Ed, stop it. You're twisting the facts.'

'You started it,' he grinned, not looking in the least abashed.

'Mr Stanwood is a friend of mine,' Issy told the two stewards who were now looking bemused, 'but I'm not part of any case.'

'That's what they all say.' Ed crossed

his arms in a gesture of confrontation, a smug smile on his face.

'Neither am I wanted for questioning.'

'I want to question you,' Ed said.

'You can stay, Mr Stanwood,' the senior of the two stewards informed him, while the other cast Issy a suspicious look, as if she didn't quite believe in her innocence. 'On the understanding there's no further trouble.'

'Scout's honour.' Ed sketched a salute.

'That was way out of order,' Issy hissed over the excited buzz of conversation around them.

'I only wanted an answer,' Ed protested.

'What was the question?' Issy asked in confusion.

'Will you marry me?'

'Certainly not.'

'Steady,' Ed warned, casting an anxious glance in the direction of the galley, 'keep your voice down. We've been told we're for the high jump if we cause any more trouble.'

'I am merely answering your question. Now will you please leave me alone?'

'I suppose I couldn't persuade you to reconsider?'

'No.'

'That's a pity, because I've promised Lucinda I'll be her spokesperson for this new scholarship thingy you're setting up in Don's name.'

'How do you know about that?'

'She sent me a text. She seems to think we're an item, and I hated to disillusion her, so I accepted the commission.' Ed tapped the side of his nose. 'I've got myself rooms in the centre of Cork and loads of new contacts. The world of journalism is far-reaching. Everyone knows someone who knows someone.'

'You're moving to Ireland?'

'Didn't I just say that?' Ed replied.

'Why?'

Ed raised his eyebrows. 'At times you can be so tiresome. All right, I'll let you have your moment of glory. On reflection, I decided I couldn't live without you; and if I wanted to spend the rest of my life with you, I was going to have to do it on your terms. As you wouldn't move across the pond, I decided I would. It was the only course of action I could take.'

'Why do you want to spend the rest of your life with me?' Issy was still in a daze and not entirely sure what was happening to her.

'Good question.'

'Then answer it,' Issy insisted.

'I happen to think you're amazing. You've taken no end of blows and never flinched. You're resourceful, kind and beautiful; and, like I told you, I want to spend the rest of my life with you. Will that do?'

'Ed, everyone's listening,' Issy whispered, aware all conversation around them had now ceased.

'I've just asked this lady to marry me,' Ed informed the nearest neighbours. 'I'm waiting for her reply.'

'Put him out of his misery, love,' a man called out, 'then we can all get some peace.'

The cabin fell quiet.

'Issy?' Ed coaxed, 'I know I can be impossible at times, and I admit I deceived you in the beginning regarding Jonathan, but I do love you. If it helps my case, I have to tell you that Cordelia would never forgive me if I let you slip through my fingers. She thinks you're the best thing that's ever happened to me.'

'She does?' Issy asked softly.

'She does,' Ed confirmed. 'So,' he asked after a pause, 'what's your answer?'

It seemed as if the cabin held its breath waiting for Issy's reply.

'It's yes,' she said softly.

'She said yes,' the neighbour shouted and got to his feet.

As cheers and applause broke and Ed leaned forward to kiss Issy, there was the pop of a champagne cork from the galley.